GAME ON

GAME ON

a VARSITY novel

by Melanie Spring

poppy

Little, Brown and Company
New York   Boston

Poppy

Hachette Book Group
237 Park Avenue, New York, NY 10017
Visit our website at www.lb-teens.com

Poppy is an imprint of Little, Brown and Company.
The Poppy name and logo are trademarks of Hachette Book Group, Inc.

The publisher is not responsible for websites (or their content) that are not owned by the publisher.

First Edition: September 2013

Library of Congress Cataloging-in-Publication Data

Spring, Melanie.
  Game on : a Varsity novel / by Melanie Spring. — First edition.
    pages cm
  Summary: "Four fourteen-year-old girls in Southern California join their school's JV cheerleading squad, preparing for the Regional cheerleading competitions while tackling the high school dramas of freshman year, first boyfriends, and the dynamics of teen-girl friendships"— Provided by publisher.
  ISBN 978-0-316-22727-8 (pbk.)
  [1. Cheerleading—Fiction.   2. Best friends—Fiction.   3. Friendship—Fiction.   4. High schools—Fiction.   5. Schools—Fiction.]   I. Title.
  PZ7.S76843Gam 2013
  [Fic]—dc23

                                                                                      2012048436

10 9 8 7 6 5 4 3 2 1

RRD-C

Printed in the United States of America

To girls with spirit everywhere

CHAPTER 1

"Come on, Kate! You can do it! Keep those knees locked tight!" Chloe Davis shouted from across the gym as Kate MacDonald landed on the mat with a thud. Kate had been trying to perfect her double toe touch all summer. She was tall and thin—what her mom called "gangly"—with dark skin. With legs as long as Kate's, it seemed like it would be easy to spring up and hit the move on the first try. But Kate had never been the most graceful girl on the squad.

For the past three months, Kate had been determined to get everything right. She had practiced her jumps all over Sunny Valley—at the beach, in her backyard on the trampoline, and at cheer camp last month with her new teammates. Kate was in awe of how Chloe made it look so effortless. After jogging in place for a few seconds, Kate prepped again for another attempt, raising her arms to a high V position. She sprang into the air. *One! Two! Clean finish.* Much better. Practice hadn't even started yet, and she was already starting to feel the burn. She had to admit, it felt really good.

"That's it!" Chloe smiled, all teeth, as she bounded over to Kate. Chloe's strawberry-blond ponytail swung behind her head. It seemed to glow under the harsh yellow lights of the gym.

"Did you feel the difference that time? You're seriously so close to perfection on that double toe touch, it's scary," Chloe said as she patted Kate on the back. "You got this."

"Thanks," Kate replied, allowing herself to grin a little. "But I think I still have a long way to go before I can get it to look like yours."

"Don't be ridiculous!" Chloe said. "We have all season to work on it before Regionals. You'll have it by then, for sure."

Kate nodded, her confidence rising. Now that she and her two best friends were on the Northside High School Junior Varsity cheer squad, it seemed especially important to get everything right. The three of them—Kate, Chloe, and Emily—had been looking forward to cheering for the Northside Timberwolves since the moment they picked up their first poms together in the sixth grade. After school, they would go over to Chloe's house and spend hours in her backyard on her giant trampoline. Chloe's older brother and sister—already on the Varsity team themselves—would teach the girls elaborate cheers that made no sense but were incredibly fun. They gave every performance their all right from the start, even if the only member of the audience was Chloe's dog, Valentine.

But they'd come a long way since Jefferson Middle School and messing around on the trampoline. The high school division was where it got really fired up, both on the field and at competitions. It was going to be intense and Kate couldn't wait. Neither could the rest of her new JV teammates. It was only the first day of practice, but Regionals were in November and she knew how quickly the time would fly.

Chloe thrived on pressure and was excited to get started. She launched her body into a perfectly executed double toe touch, followed by a standing back tuck.

"That looked sooo amazing," a petite girl with large blue eyes said in awe as Chloe shook out her muscles after the trick.

"Thanks, Lexi! Your back handsprings are looking really solid lately, too."

"You think so?" Lexi replied, smiling shyly. "It feels like they are my worst skill."

Chloe shook her head in protest. "No way! Ever since we practiced them at camp, you've improved so much." Chloe smiled warmly. She was the definition of a great cheerleader—especially when it came to encouraging other members of her own squad. That's why she was almost everyone's top pick for JV captain this year. The fact that she was also an extremely talented tumbler didn't hurt her chances, either. Chloe's round-off back tuck was textbook, and, naturally, everyone wanted her help on how to nail their own skills.

After chatting with Lexi for another minute, Chloe made her way back to Kate's spot, where their friend Emily Arellano joined them.

"You guys want to grab a water before practice starts?" Chloe asked. "I'm already thirsty." Chloe tightened her high ponytail and smoothed down the fabric of her brand-new NHS Cheer cotton tee.

Emily started stretching her hamstrings in a front pike position on the floor. Her dark hair was also pulled up, away from her face. Emily was blessed with a perpetually clear complexion, long eyelashes, and olive skin that didn't require much makeup. "That's probably a good idea. I *swear* I've sweated out half of my electrolytes from nerves alone," she said. Emily sniffed her underarm warily. "Oh, man, do I already smell? Kate, smell me."

"I absolutely will not!" Kate laughed, swatting away the armpit Emily had presented to her.

"What about you, Chloe?" Emily asked. Chloe responded by scrunching up her small nose.

"What is wrong with you people? That's the smell of success!" Emily giggled, putting her hands on her hips triumphantly like Peter Pan. Her friends laughed, but there were still no takers.

"That's cool. You guys probably won't be able to avoid it once you're lifting me into a heel stretch later. The perks of being a top girl. Everyone all up in your business all the time... Only Kalyn and Lexi can truly understand my pain," Emily joked, referring to the other two top girls on the squad—Kalyn Min and Lexi Foster.

"I'm so glad I'm a base," Kate agreed. It took a special breed of girl to be brave enough to take the top position. But every position on the team had its advantages, along with its challenges. All of them were necessary to keep the team performing stunts like a complex machine.

"Come on, we only have a few minutes. We can't be late on the first day or Coach Steele will make an example of us," Chloe urged as she led the way toward a vending machine just outside the gym. "And trust me, that is something we *don't* want," she added.

Emily and Kate fell in line behind Chloe. Coach Steele

was a great coach, but pretty strict about certain things like tardiness. Chloe loved her friends, but she wasn't going to let them get her in trouble. Not today. It was way too important.

"Copy that," said Kate as they reached the glowing vending machine. She hunched over to drop some quarters into the slot, and made her selection. "Can you get a demerit for being tardy?" she asked. It was as if Chloe had told her they were already in trouble. Kate was obsessed with demerits—the negative point system used by cheerleaders everywhere when squad members violated the Cheerleader Contract. It was common knowledge that they could get demerits for offenses ranging from minor ones, such as wearing press-on nails, to major ones, like being caught drinking at a party. The toughest rule for some of the girls to follow was that they couldn't be seen making any physical contact with boys while in uniform—no hand-holding, no hugging, and especially no kissing. Anyone who earned enough demerits was automatically kicked off the squad. Kate's eyes grew wide as she turned to Chloe. "Did your brother or sister ever get any?" she asked.

"Clem never did," Chloe answered, shrugging. "She was the perfect Northside cheerleader. But I think Jake got a few that time his friends made him streak across campus for losing a bet."

"But it's not like they were gonna kick *him* off the

squad," Emily added, hitting the machine to try to make an extra water bottle fall out. Her attempt didn't work.

Chloe's two older siblings, Jake and Clementine Davis, were legends at Northside High. Her brother had originally been on the football team and had led the school to victory at State Championships during his junior year. Clementine had been on the Varsity cheerleading squad, which at the time was struggling and in need of strong bases for stunts. Clementine begged Jake to join the squad, and he shocked everyone by leaving the football team behind and taking his place on the sidelines instead. He had always been the type of guy to do his own thing. And, just like Chloe, he had undeniable charisma.

He had so much influence, in fact, that several other guys had followed his lead and joined the squad, which led to the most successful cheerleading season in NHS history. Even though Chloe had only been in fifth grade, watching her siblings perform and compete had made her fall in love with Northside. There was even a picture hanging in the hallway at Chloe's house of her at age ten, wearing a blue-and-gold T-shirt that said FUTURE NHS CHEERLEADER. Her status as part of the "Davis Dynasty" allowed her some valuable insider knowledge about the cheerleading program at Northside. There was no doubt that Chloe was prepped for success on this team.

By the time they got back to the gym, it had filled with

other girls on the squad. Idle chatter about the upcoming football season and cute upperclassmen echoed throughout the room. There was a buzz in the air that went beyond even the pumped-up spirit they'd felt at camp last month. Maybe it was because they were finally in their own gym, on their home turf. The blue-and-gold lettering on the wall proudly proclaimed that they were in TIMBERWOLF TERRITORY!

"I'm gonna go say hi to Carley and Jenn," Chloe said as two more girls entered the gym. Carley Chase-Calloway, a tall brunette with coffee-colored skin and almond-shaped eyes, and Jenn Hoffheimer, a short blond with a spray of freckles across her nose, dropped their bags on the bleachers. The two were decked out in their royal-blue cheer shorts and camp spirit shirts that read NORTHSIDE on the front and TEAMWORK MAKES THE DREAM WORK in glittery gold letters on the back. "Hey, girls!" Chloe shouted, giving them a wave. "Isn't this exciting?" she chirped.

"I swear, that girl is a natural," Emily observed as Chloe greeted the newcomers. A few more girls had entered the gym and started to gather around Chloe, who was now telling an animated story about something funny that had happened during lunch.

"There is no way Chloe won't make captain, right?" Emily added with a slight grin, her dark eyes twinkling with excitement about everything going on around her. She bent down to touch the floor and stretch her hamstrings some more. Emily was so flexible, she could place her face completely on her shins without wincing.

"Of course she'll be captain. Everyone loves Chloe." Kate shrugged, watching as Chloe drew Jenn into a warm and genuine embrace. "Look at her. Chloe Davis—cheerleader of the people!" Kate said with admiration.

Even though many of the other girls on the squad had come from the town's other middle school, Los Gatos, they had quickly bonded as a team. Camp had made sure of that—long days spent together learning new stunts and cheers in workshops followed by nights in the bunks laughing until they fell asleep, their muscles so achy that soreness seemed like a permanent state of being.

The only one who didn't look pleased to see Chloe was Leila Savett, a lanky brunette and fellow base, who stood with her arms crossed and a trademark sneer on her face. Her long, shiny hair was still down around her shoulders. She always waited until the last second to put it up in a ponytail so that it didn't "crease as much."

Leila threw her duffel bag on the ground and sat down on a mat to start stretching, like it was a chore. She looked at Chloe and narrowed her kohl-lined eyes. The look was meant to be intimidating, but it didn't faze Chloe—she'd known Leila and her competitive streak since elementary school. It was weird to think that they used to be such close friends. Friends who carpooled to Sunny Valley All-Stars, the cheerleading gym where they trained on the weekends. Friends who would get smoothies together at the snack bar. And, once in a while, friends who would sleep over at each other's houses.

But when Chloe advanced to the elite team and Leila didn't, something changed. Leila no longer wanted to be friendly. She took Chloe's achievement personally and responded by working extra-hard to get to the same level as Chloe—putting in tons of time at the gym and signing up for private tumbling lessons. Chloe respected Leila for working so hard, but even though Leila's cheerleading had improved, her attitude had not.

The girls' coach, Meg Steele, sat on the freshman bleachers, watching over the gym like a queen on her throne. She wore navy warm-ups with a gold stripe accent down the sleeves of the jacket, and a brand-new pair of running sneakers. Tortoiseshell sunglasses sat pushed back on her head, causing a few pieces of her short brown hair to stick out in various directions. She sipped from a stainless-steel coffee thermos as she surveyed the squad. Even though she was in her midforties, Coach Steele could almost pass for a high school cheerleader herself. Only the deep laugh lines around her eyes—the result of years of smiling while shouting cheers—gave away her age.

The girls loved how the coach could joke around but would also display tough love when it came to training them for competition. They knew she wanted to bring out the best in her squad. The Varsity team had already warned the JV girls that there was a time for messing around and a time to work. If they wanted to get on Coach Steele's good side, they would learn the difference—fast.

Coach Steele was furiously scribbling something on her clipboard—probably the agenda for today's practice. Every day before practice, she liked to come up with an action plan. Coach Steele reminded her squads that cheerleaders are athletes, just like football players. If the football team went over plays before practice, why shouldn't the cheerleaders also have a plan of action for each practice and game? Emily hoped today's action plan included cradles so she could attempt a full down again. There was nothing like the rush that accompanied a perfectly executed stunt. Of course, that was probably too advanced for day one.

"Who's that?" Kate asked, squinting and gesturing toward the bleachers.

Emily scanned the group. "Coach Steele?"

"No, her!" Kate said, pointing to the top row. The girl in question had her head down and her legs propped up on the bench, bouncing nervously.

"I have no idea. I thought this was a closed practice," Emily said, shrugging. "And it's not like she's on the team."

Tryouts had been held back in May, after all. Not one of the final squad members could forget that grueling week of learning routines and stunts, then having to perform them before a panel of judges. But that was the deal. It had to be tough enough to weed out the candidates who just liked the idea of wearing a cute uniform. Cheerleading wasn't something you decided to do on a whim—it required hard work and dedication. *Passion.*

Coach Steele smoothed her hair and blew her whistle. "Good afternoon, my lovely Junior Varsity TIM-BER-WOOOOLVES!" she hollered as if it were its own cheer. "Please gather 'round, ladies!" Everyone obliged, forming a huge circle around her. Kate and Emily hung back, and Chloe joined them. "I know you're all excited about your first official practice of the season, so I'll make this as brief as possible. First off, I want to welcome you all to Northside. I know we are going to have a thrilling year cheering at games and pep rallies, practicing hard, and competing together. As long as you all follow the contract you signed when you became a part of this team, we should have a great season. You should all be very proud of yourselves—you are the cream of the crop and are all very talented athletes to have made it this far. I'm lucky to have every one of you here. Give yourselves a hand, ladies!" Coach Steele smiled and started clapping her hands together above her head.

Everyone started to whistle and clap.

"Okay, okay. Now, calm yourselves for a moment—I have an important announcement." Chloe fidgeted. This was it. The moment she'd been waiting for all day. She reached over and squeezed Emily's hand for support.

"As some of you may have noticed, we have a new face among us today," Coach Steele said as she looked around at each of the girls. Chloe didn't notice any new faces. She looked at Emily in confusion. Emily shrugged. "I know I normally don't allow any extra visitors at practice, but I want you all to give a warm *Timberwolf* welcome to Miss Devin Isle!"

The girl from the bleachers stood up timidly and made her way to Coach Steele's side. She and Coach Steele exchanged a quick, knowing glance. But with her wide-eyed expression, her insane red curls, and her outfit, Devin looked out of place in the crowd of cheerleaders. While most of the other girls wore new shorts, NHS T-shirts, and shiny white ribbons in their ponytails, Devin was sporting an old Hanes tee, boys' soccer shorts, and tattered running shoes. Not the best look.

Chloe released Emily's hand. That wasn't the announcement she'd been expecting. She thought they were going to hear about the upcoming vote for captain of the squad, not about some random girl who would be training with them. A quick look around the room confirmed that Chloe wasn't the only one confused about the unexpected visitor. Several girls began whispering to one another. Kate furrowed her brow in her usual quiet and concerned manner.

Coach Steele held her hands in front of her to stop the commotion. "Quiet down, girls. Devin just moved from the Bay Area. Her sister, Sage, was one of my star cheerleaders a few years ago. Now, Devin's not a cheerleader, but my girl here has some serious gymnastics skills and needs to take them for a spin today. So please be extra-nice! If everything goes well today, Devin may become your newest teammate, and I'm asking that you all treat her like she's already part of the squad."

Devin forced a weak smile, clearly embarrassed to be presented to the group in such a fashion. She put her hand up to wave hello.

"Great. Just what we need. Someone else to be given special treatment because of her family," Leila muttered under her breath. Marcy Martinez, a short, sturdy girl with jet-black hair, shook her head in mutual disgust. Emily often referred to her as Savett's Shadow because she never left Leila's side and always sought her approval. Leila was known for making comments that Chloe was only on the team because of the "Davis Dynasty." Leila just didn't want to believe that anyone else could be a great cheerleader in her own right or that rewards were merit-based. Anyone with eyes could see that Chloe was talented, regardless of her last name.

"*Sage Isle?*" Kate whispered to Chloe. "Didn't she compete against your brother and sister at Nationals? I think I saw a spotlight article on her once in *American Cheerleader* magazine."

Chloe knew that name had sounded familiar. She suddenly felt her heart drop into her stomach as a memory of a tall, strong redhead doing a full twisting layout tumbled through her mind. Sage Isle had definitely competed against Jake and Clementine the year they'd cheered together. That red hair was unmistakable, and she had been incredible. Chloe studied the girl in front of her, who was meekly staring at the floor and shuffling around nervously. Coach Steele was definitely up to something, Chloe realized, and she didn't have a good feeling about it.

CHAPTER 2

"You look really pale, Chlo," Emily whispered. "Are you okay?"

Chloe realized she wasn't breathing.

"Don't worry. Look at her outfit. She couldn't care less about cheerleading," Emily continued, under her breath.

Chloe took in the sight of Devin—all wide-eyed and messy. Emily was right. Why was she being so paranoid?

Coach Steele continued talking. "Now, before we get started on our basic tumbling passes, I have one more very important order of business to address." Coach Steele paused for dramatic effect. "I'm talking about the vote for captain." She put her hands on her hips and began to pace back and forth while she spoke to the group. Electing a captain was a serious topic. Chloe clenched her jaw as she listened.

"You all may be aware that we elect our captains a little differently at Northside High. For those of you who don't know," the coach said, turning to Devin, "I'll break it down. Just like the scoring system at competition, it's a combination of a few different things. First and foremost, your ability to lead the team, in the eyes of your peers. Are you dedicated to the team? Do you embody the true spirit of a Northside Timberwolf? Do you set a good example for everyone else on the squad and in the student body? That is where the team vote comes in." Chloe looked around at her peers, trying to decide whether she'd proven her ability to lead. Jenn smiled back at her reassuringly, and Chloe's confidence went up.

Coach Steele continued to pace around the group as she spoke, her sneakers squeaking on the gym floor. "But equally important are your unique talents and strengths as seen by your coach." She pointed to herself as she said this. "You've all gotten to know one another pretty well over the summer, so it shouldn't be too hard to decide who you want to represent you. I want each of you to make your decision and e-mail it to me by Thursday afternoon. I will then weigh your votes against my own evaluations and announce the new JV captain at the first game of the season, against Medham on Friday."

"Coach?" Marcy raised her hand.

"Yes, Martinez?" Coach Steele replied, stopping directly in front of her.

"Can we nominate people? Because I'd like to nominate Leila Savett," Marcy said with a smile, looking around at her teammates. Leila wore a smug expression as Marcy spoke in her fast, high-pitched voice. "She has the most cheerleading experience out of anyone on the team. And since *everyone* at NHS likes Leila, I think she could get a lot more students involved in spirit activities this year."

"Oh, please," Jenn muttered under her breath.

Coach Steele could see where this was going. "Marcy, we don't really have time to—"

Emily scoffed audibly and didn't bother to raise her hand before interrupting Coach Steele. "Well, if we're just throwing names out there, I'd like to say that *I'm* voting for Chloe Davis. Because she would *actually* be a good captain."

A few other girls nodded in agreement.

"Wow, I'm so totally hurt by that," Leila replied, rolling her eyes. "Or I would be if your opinion mattered to me at all."

Emily ignored her and kept talking. "Also, Marcy was wrong when she said that Leila has the most experience. Chloe has been cheerleading for just as long."

Coach Steele held up a hand to stop Emily and interrupted her speech. "Ladies, that's enough. This is not a contest of who has been training longer—it's about who will make the best captain." The coach's voice turned serious and the girls grew silent. "And no more campaigning. Just send me your votes and we will find out soon enough."

Leila nudged Marcy and started whispering something to her. Judging by Leila's exasperated expression, their plan for an impromptu debate had gone awry. Marcy frowned and slumped down. She would probably never hear the end of this from Leila.

Coach Steele clapped her hands together. "All right, now that that's all out of the way, let's get this party started! Ten laps around the gym and twenty push-ups. And if any of you stop to look at a cell phone during practice, that's twenty more!" Coach Steele pointed directly at Leila. "I mean it, Savett." Leila responded with a pouty look, but the coach had already turned away.

"Let's go!" Chloe shouted. A couple of the girls started clapping and whistling.

"Tim-ber! Tim-ber! Tim-ber!" Emily shouted as she began a lap.

"WOLVES!" the whole squad shouted in response, circling the perimeter of the gym. Everyone's spirits were high and their voices loud. Everyone's, Chloe noticed, except Devin's. Maybe she didn't know she was supposed to shout back, or maybe she just didn't care.

"Wolves!" Devin squeaked a second too late, running alone in the back, but her voice went unnoticed.

Maybe it was the endorphins, but fifteen minutes later, Chloe was starting to feel much more like herself—confident and happy. After the laps and push-ups, Coach Steele had made the girls run relays across the gym. Then she had them do a short round of conditioning, followed by a series of jumps: side hurdlers, toe touches, and pikes. When it wasn't her turn to go, Chloe liked to observe the others' technique, mentally filing away their strengths and weaknesses. She kept an especially watchful eye on Devin. The frazzled redhead didn't seem excited to be there at all. She looked distant, like her mind was miles away.

At that low energy level, Devin never even would have made it past the first round of cheerleading tryouts back in the spring. Chloe silently wondered what the point was of her being there to practice with them. She was just some gymnast. Maybe Coach Steele felt bad for the poor girl because Devin was new in town. The coach always did have a soft spot for underdogs. It was why she had originally come to coach at Northside. The head coach at the time, Coach Steele's old friend and teammate Bryan Regan, had left to coach at Northside's biggest rival, Breckenridge High School. Northside had been a mess, but Coach Steele had brought the team up to elite status within a few seasons.

The coach unzipped her hoodie and threw it toward the bleachers as the girls finished a short combination of jumps.

She fanned herself with the action-plan paper and motioned for them to stop. The gym was actually getting a little steamy from the intense activity. "Okay, girls. Let's get to some basic tumbling. I want you lined up in groups of three by the mats. We'll start with some round-offs, but you are free to modify it with a tuck on your second pass. Don't push it. I don't want any injuries on the first day. Or any day, for that matter! Only if you feel ready."

Chloe had never been more ready. She didn't even wait for her second pass—she went full out into a round-off, back handspring, back tuck. It felt amazing, and she stood up straight with a smile.

Suddenly, she was brought back down to earth. "Chloe—I said *second* pass!" Coach Steele chided, shaking her head. Chloe brushed off the coach's reprimand and scanned the room to see whether any of her teammates had seen her near-perfect execution, hoping for some sort of acknowledgment. But it seemed their eyes were glued to something else.

Chloe watched as a flash of red curls darted past. Devin flew through the air, executing a perfect round-off, back handspring, into a layout. Even her landing was clean. The squad erupted in applause and whistles.

"Ow-ow-ow!" Carley hollered, jumping up and down in excitement. Emily's jaw dropped and she looked toward Chloe. Chloe couldn't believe her eyes.

"Way to go, Devin!" Coach Steele shouted, grinning from ear to ear. Devin began to flush a shade brighter than her hair. She took a quick, self-deprecating bow and ambled awkwardly to the back of the group. Coach Steele patted Devin on the shoulder and blew her whistle to quiet the room from the excitement. "Let's focus, ladies!"

Leila suddenly appeared at Chloe's side, looking a little too pleased. "Guess you and I have some new competition." Then Leila turned on her heel, Marcy in tow. Chloe watched them jog over to Devin and give her high fives.

"Nice to finally get someone else with talent around here!" Leila said to Devin loudly, to make sure Chloe heard. "Are you joining the team? I have basically been carrying this group all summer and could use the help."

"That was increds," Marcy said. "Can you teach me how to do that?"

"Me too!" said Jenn. "I really want to learn a layout this season."

Chloe watched in horror as a few more girls hovered around Devin like she was going to whip out a marker and start signing autographs.

Chloe walked over to Kate and Emily. "You guys? She's not that good, right?" Chloe asked, hoping for some reassurance. "Right?"

But Emily and Kate didn't respond—they just stared ahead in mutual shock.

Chloe didn't know much about her, but she did know one thing for sure: Devin Isle wasn't just some girl with bad workout clothes. She was a super-skilled athlete, cheerleader or not. And the way the whole squad was falling all over themselves to talk to her made Chloe feel shaky, like someone was pulling the cheer mat right out from under her.

CHAPTER 3

Devin had moved the poster of Gabby Douglas
three times now, hoping to cover some of the spots on the
wall where the ugly floral wallpaper had begun to peel. But
the poster didn't look right anywhere. Devin ripped it
down in exasperation. It was better to not even try. She was
just trying to make it look like her old room in Spring Park,
but she wasn't there. She was here, in Sunny Valley, and she
felt like an impostor in her own life. Especially after today
and the bizarre experience of cheerleading practice.

Devin had felt so out of place standing there in front of
the Northside squad that afternoon. Her first day of school
had been hectic enough—not knowing anyone or where

any of her classes were. By the end of the day, all she felt like doing was going home, curling up in her bed with her fluffy orange cat, Emerald, and falling asleep. But she had promised Coach Steele that she'd come by the gym after school. Devin and her mom had gotten to know Meg Steele back when she was coaching Devin's older sister, Sage, in Spring Park. Just yesterday, the coach had stopped by their new house to see how they were settling in and, apparently, to recruit Devin.

When Coach Steele made her announcement at practice, the girls of the Northside High cheerleading team seemed to have been surprised to see an outsider. Their expressions were mostly a mixture of excitement and curiosity, but one girl, Chloe, had looked almost hurt and maybe even a little angry. For some reason, that had made Devin want to prove herself. She suddenly wanted to show everyone that her skills were equal to, or even better than, those of the girls already on the squad. She'd shown off during tumbling and now realized they probably all thought she was full of herself. Devin's cheeks felt hot with embarrassment just thinking about it.

Devin collapsed onto her bed. It was made up with the new plum-colored duvet set her mom had bought her as a peace offering. The fabric was gorgeous and soft, but it didn't make up for the fact that her mom had uprooted Devin's whole life by moving them hundreds of miles away from everything and everyone Devin cared about. *Except Sage*, she reminded herself. Now entering her sophomore year at UCLA, Devin's big sister was only about forty-five minutes away. At least that's what her mom had claimed in the pitch to move down here. So far, though, Sage had only visited a couple of times. Devin knew that Sage was busy with summer classes and training on the UCLA cheer team, but she still felt a little cheated.

Devin stared at the framed picture of her family—the four of them, back when they were still a complete unit. Innocent Devin stared back at her. She was smiling wide, squashed between her parents, totally unaware of what was about to happen to her life. Sage had handled the divorce better than Devin, but that was mainly because she was about to escape to college, where she could ignore it all. Not that Devin blamed Sage for that—Devin often wished that she could run away, too, to somewhere new and exciting. A place that had nothing to do with her messed-up home life. Maybe New York City, maybe Hawaii. Just anywhere else that was far, far away.

But when her mother first broke the news that the two of them were moving down to Southern California from the Bay Area, Devin immediately regretted wishing so hard for an escape. In reality, it meant that she would have to leave behind her two crazy but lovable best friends, Nina James and Cameron Woodard; her home gym, Rocket

Gymnastics; and—worst of all—her adorable boyfriend of six months, Josh Griffith. It was embarrassing for an independent girl like Devin to admit, but leaving Josh had been the hardest part of the move. He was smart, funny, and completely unlike any other boys her age. Also, he was incredibly cute and played guitar, which only increased his appeal. All these epic life changes made her feel dizzier than performing her floor routine for a packed house during a gymnastics meet.

Devin forced herself up from her cushy safe haven. She was already starting to feel sore from practice and it took extra effort. There was no use lying around moping. Plus, her mom would be home any minute from a grueling shift at Sunny Valley County Hospital. No doubt Linda Isle would be ravenous and grumpy.

Devin positioned her body in front of her full-length, gold-framed mirror. She weakly clapped her hands twice. "N-H-S!" she said, but it was barely audible. "Yell N-H-S!" she yelled a bit louder. *Man, this feels ridiculous.* "YOU LOOK DUMB!" she shouted at her reflection. *That's more accurate*, she thought. It was no use.

Emerald wove around her ankles, purring. "Hello, my little motor. You hungry?" She picked up her fuzzy orange cat and rubbed her under the chin. "Probably time to start dinner for us humans, too."

Since she and her mom had moved, Devin usually

made dinner for the two of them. Nothing too fancy—just chicken and rice pilaf or spaghetti with meat sauce. Devin found cooking sort of relaxing, as far as chores went. Plus, there was always a lot to do around the house, and Devin felt obligated to help out, even if she was still bitter about their new situation in Sunny Valley.

The divorce had been hard on everyone, but her mom seemed especially different now, like a sad, defeated version of her former self. Devin still thought her parents could have worked it out, if only they'd tried a little harder. Instead, they'd given up. It was disheartening for a girl who had been taught to never give up on anything. "Just stick it out and everything will be fine," her parents would say. *Good advice, guys*, Devin thought.

An old laptop hummed on Devin's desk. She unplugged the cord and carried it downstairs. Having it with her while she cooked made her feel slightly less alone. Emerald meowing at her feet also helped. She had just opened a can of wet cat food and put a pot of water on the stove to boil, when she heard the alert of an instant message from the computer speaker.

sixstringJOSH: hey there hot stuff. u come here often?

Devin walked over to the laptop to write back.

theDevver: u could say I'm a regular. :)
sixstringJOSH: can I interest u in a
root beer and a song?
theDevver: course!

Devin opened the fridge and grabbed a can of root beer, popping the tab and taking a quick sip before the video chat window rang. When she clicked it, there was Josh, sitting in his messy bedroom back home. Nothing had changed. His bed was still unmade and there were dirty clothes strewn everywhere. Same dark, tanned skin, same light blue eyes, and his smile was as wide as ever.

"Devver!" he exclaimed. "You ready?" Devin could see the strap of his acoustic guitar, which he called Lucy, for reasons unknown. The strap was covered with patches, including one she'd gotten for him right before she moved. It was a yellow star, edged in black. Hearts weren't really their thing.

"Cheers!" She raised her soda can in a salute, and he did the same with an identical can. They sipped in unison.

Josh then began a song he said was called "Devin, How Was Your Day? Mine Sucked (Without You)." He sang about how much he missed her and about how he had been assigned to do a semester-long biology project with the class mean girl, Stephanie von Tresser. Devin also learned that he'd eaten two bean burritos for lunch and that his friend Luke was joining the football team.

"Can you believe he's selling out like that?" Josh asked, draining his soda can. "I will never understand these people. Putting on a ridiculous uniform in the school colors and acting like it's some big honorable thing."

"Yeah…pretty stupid." Devin froze. "But it could be cool to be a part of a team or something. Maybe."

"What? No way. School sports are so annoying. And since you left, the only person who will ditch pep rallies with me is Jeremy. Come baaaack. Spring Park sucks without the Devver."

"You're right. School sports are lame," Devin replied, and forced a laugh. She wondered if he could read the guilty look on her face. It wasn't like she'd really done anything wrong. She had just gone to a Northside cheerleading practice. Once. To please her mom and Coach Steele. It wasn't like she was really joining the team. Josh would never even have to know about her little foray into the school-spirit world.

"So how is the new school, Red? Make any friends?"

She propped the camera so she could cook as they chatted, and started to heat up some marinara sauce in a pan.

"It's all right, but it's no Spring Park. They don't even have any film electives. I'm stuck taking ceramics. And you know how much I suck at studio art."

"You do suck at art," Josh joked. "But I like you anyway."

"Oh, thanks!" Devin said, laughing. Man, she missed him a lot.

"Did you look for any new gyms? It's been a while, Dev." He strummed the strings of his guitar lazily.

"I told you—the closest one is thirty minutes away. I don't want to stress my mom out any more than she already is." Devin dumped the cooked pasta into a strainer and yelled across the kitchen. "It's not like she has any extra time to drive me to practices. She worked three double shifts this week. Not to mention the gym fees..."

"I know. I just want to see you happy. Back-flipping and jumping around in really tight spandex."

"Keyword: *spandex*." Devin smiled and rolled her eyes at him. *Boys*. "I think that's what makes *you* happy."

The sound of a car pulling up outside signaled her mom's arrival.

"Well, I'm not saying it doesn't, but..."

"Ack! Gotta go, Josh. Miss you."

"Later, Devver. Miss you, too. Tune in tomorrow for another thrilling song!"

"Can't wait."

She blew him a quick kiss and waved good-bye.

"And this one will actually be composed beforehand," he added with a wink, before the video screen went black.

He was so sweet to her. Maybe she should have just told him about the cheer practice. It was the first time she'd ever kept a secret like that from one of their chats. After the whole Luke/team-sports thing, she had been afraid of what he'd say.

"Smells great!" Linda Isle said, entering the kitchen and collapsing into a chair at the dining table. She still had her scrubs on. Today they were blue, with pink Cheshire cats on them. Devin had chosen them for her a few years ago, so the smiling cats were really faded. The idea of faded smiles made Devin kind of depressed.

"I'm absolutely starving. How did you know, honey?"

"You're always hungry, Mom."

"And in need of wine."

Linda got up and poured herself a glass as Devin carried the bowls of pasta and sauce over to the table.

"Rough day. One of the kids in the PICU gave me a hell of a time when I was trying to give him his afternoon meds. Pulled the IV straight out of his arm and started screaming at a pitch I didn't know existed." She took a sip of wine. "So how was school today?" her mom asked, trying to sound casual. "I hope everything went well. Did you go see Coach Steele? About the team? It's so lucky that she coaches at Northside—I could hardly believe how perfect it was when I found out. I thought we'd lost her for good when she left Spring Park."

Devin took a massive bite of pasta to buy herself a few moments before she had to answer. She knew that she should break the news that she wasn't actually joining the squad, but her mom looked so tired. And sad . . . with faded smiles all over her shirt.

"Yeah, I went," Devin offered, and took another bite.

A look of hope flashed over her mom's face. "You did? How was it?" As soon as Devin saw her look so happy—happier than she'd been in months—she didn't want to be the one to ruin it. Devin took a swig of root beer, wiped her face, and decided that it was probably better to be honest.

"I'm not sure, Mom," she replied hesitantly.

"Look, I know it's not ideal," Linda replied, her expression turning. "I know you'd rather be back at Rocket, practicing your beam routine with the old gang. But you might make some new friends on the cheerleading team here! And you'll be able to keep up your tumbling skills until we can sort out something else. . . ." She raised her eyebrows expectantly, like it was the best suggestion in the world.

Devin put her head in her hands. She hated conversations like this—where her mom had already made her mind up for the both of them but tried to present it like Devin had a choice in the matter. "Mom, I told you I never wanted to do cheerleading again, after what happened." Devin took out her aggression on a piece of bread and dipped it in some marinara sauce.

"Oh, honey," Linda said through a mouthful of pasta. "Honestly, I don't know why you're still bothered by that.

A lot of people don't make the Bay Elite All-Stars on their first try. Sage was an exception to the rule. You would have made it if you'd tried again. You know—"

"But I didn't want to try again," Devin interrupted. "And I don't want to now. I want to do gymnastics. I want to be back at home, in the Bay. With Dad. And Josh." She twirled a noodle around her fork, avoiding eye contact as she said it.

Linda grew quiet. Devin had touched a raw nerve. She instantly realized she'd gone too far by mentioning her dad. After a few excruciating moments of silence, her mom finally spoke. "I know it's been hard, Dev. But I'm trying. It would mean a lot if you would just give it another shot. For me?"

Devin breathed a heavy sigh.

Linda reached across the table and touched Devin's hand. "Just for a bit. Okay?"

"Fine," Devin conceded. "I'll stick with it for one game. But that's it."

Her mother's face instantly relaxed and she allowed herself to smile genuinely. It made Devin feel guilty.

"Your sister is going to be thrilled! Go, Northside!" Linda pumped her fists in the air like she was holding imaginary pom-pons.

"Go, Northside," Devin replied as her mom hustled out of the room to call Sage.

Devin may have been fearless when it came to performing acrobatics, but now that it was her life that was completely flipped upside down, she was totally scared. Her humiliating failure at trying out for the elite team back home had made her swear she would never attempt cheerleading again, but deep down, a little part of her was excited about a second chance to prove herself. All she had to do now was take the leap and hope that someone would be there to spot her.

CHAPTER 4

Devin didn't mind sitting by herself at lunch. She actually enjoyed how peaceful it was to be outside under a shady tree, reading a book while she munched her turkey on rye. It was also great for ignoring the fact that she wasn't eating with Cameron, Nina, and Josh. Sadly, she also knew that if she wanted to be part of Northside's social scene at all, she'd have to make some friends soon or risk being labeled the weird loner girl. As much as she didn't really care what people thought of her, Devin wanted to avoid that image.

Devin took a bite of her yellow-and-pink Honeycrisp apple and surveyed the students around her. For the most part, they looked the same as the kids at Spring Park, standing in little cliques, drinking sodas, and gossiping. More of the girls had their hair bleached blond, and the colors of the athletes' letter jackets were blue and gold, but otherwise things were pretty similar. Devin suddenly imagined herself in a Northside cheerleading uniform. Blue would look great with her red hair, unlike the deep red color of the uniform at Spring Park. *Well, that's something,* she thought, but then immediately felt silly. She was really scraping the bottom of the barrel if that was the only good thing she could see about going to a new school and being guilt-tripped into joining cheerleading.

Devin reached into her purple canvas backpack and dug around for her phone. It was off, of course, since phones were strictly forbidden during school hours. The last thing she needed was to lose her link to her friends back home because some annoyed teacher decided to confiscate it. She smoothed her thumb over the touchscreen. Maybe it would be okay if she turned it on really fast and kept it in her bag while she texted Josh.

@ lunch right now. all alone and missin u.
drinking a root beer tho.
xx devver

It only took a few seconds for him to write back. Devin smiled as she read his reply, even though it made her heart ache.

Me too!! Lunch really sucks when I can't hug my girl.
How is ur day going? Nina says hi.

Devin looked around to make sure no one had seen her,
and started to type another message.

Hi Nina!! My day is all right—

"I'd turn that off right now if I were you," Leila said,
startling Devin. Leila had come out of nowhere and now
stood directly over her, blocking the sunlight from Devin's
place under the tree. Leila took a seat next to Devin on the
grass and pointed at Devin's backpack. "Your phone?"

"What?" Devin replied, acting innocent.

"Please," Leila said. "Give me a break. Like I care if
you're texting. I'm just trying to help you because that narc
over there is ready to pounce." Leila motioned to a campus
guard about twenty feet away. He was wearing a pair of ill-
fitting jeans, a royal-blue NHS polo, and a look of mis-
guided self-importance. Sure enough, he was staring right
at Devin.

"They have nothing better to do than bust kids for texting on campus," Leila said, flipping her shiny brown hair to
one shoulder. She looked much more polished now than at
practice the other day. She was wearing a sky-blue cap-
sleeve chiffon top that made her icy blue eyes pop, dark

skinny jeans, and gold accessories. She looked like a modern-day Princess Jasmine. "So I thought I'd save you," continued Leila as she pulled out a bottle of water and some carrot sticks.

Devin was confused by this act of kindness from a girl who'd initially seemed like such a diva. "Thanks," she said hesitantly.

"No big," Leila replied, taking a sip of water. "Who were you texting anyway? It was a guy, huh?"

Devin blushed. Leila may have just saved her from a narc, but that didn't make them close enough to exchange boy details. "It was just a friend from back home," she offered.

"A guy friend," proclaimed Leila. She raised her eyebrows deviously. "I can tell."

"Maybe…" Devin admitted, looking away. Talking about Josh with someone she hardly knew felt odd. She really wanted to change the subject. "So…how do you like Northside so far? Is high school everything you expected it to be?" Devin wasn't the best at casual conversation. She always sounded a little stiff and awkward.

"Totally!" Leila replied. "Nothing but hot guys as far as the eye can see. Plus, a cheerleading team that actually stands a chance at winning Regionals for the first time in four years. Well, if Chloe Davis doesn't become captain, that is." She bit down hard on a carrot and chewed furiously.

"Why is that?" asked Devin, genuinely intrigued. She had sensed a bit of a rivalry between the two girls the other day.

"Because," Leila explained, "she's not that great and everyone acts like she is the prodigal cheerleader or something. Just because her siblings were good, like, years ago. I'm so much better than her." Leila took another sip of water and wrinkled her nose. "Mark my words: if Chloe Davis is captain, the JV team is totally screwed this season."

"Don't you think that's a little extreme?" Devin was starting to feel bad for Chloe. "She seems... nice enough."

"Who are you voting for?" Leila said, suddenly animated.

"What do you mean? I'm not even—" Devin started to protest.

Leila cut her off. "Don't play dumb! I saw you talking to Coach Steele yesterday. I know you're joining the team." Leila smirked. "That tumbling pass you did really pissed off Chloe and her friends. Good job."

"I wasn't trying to show off," Devin said sincerely. "Really, all I wanted to do was practice some gymnastics." She was beginning to feel like she had accidentally joined a side in an old argument she knew nothing about.

"It doesn't matter what you were trying to do then," Leila said, standing up. "But it does matter what you do now." Leila reached her arm out to Devin to help her up from the grass.

"What do you mean?" Devin asked as she hesitantly accepted Leila's hand.

"I have a great idea." Leila's lips slowly formed a devilish smile. "I think that *you* should be the captain of the JV Timberwolves."

"Me?" Devin replied, incredulous. Had Leila seriously just suggested that she not only join the cheerleading team...but become captain of it? It was the most ridiculous thing Devin had heard all day—even considering she had walked in on her mom having a one-sided conversation with the cat that morning over breakfast. "There's no way. Why would you even want me to be your captain?"

"Well, honestly, *I* want to be captain," said Leila. "But the way Chloe's got everyone wrapped around her finger, including Coach Steele—"

"I don't get where I come into this," Devin interrupted drily.

"You're new and exciting," Leila said simply. "You're the only one who can beat her." Leila crossed her arms over her chest to show that she wasn't backing down. "This is perfect. You have to do it."

"That's nice and all," Devin said, slinging her backpack over her shoulder. "But I'll pass. I don't want to get in the middle of anything. I've never even cheered before, and honestly...I'm not even sure I want to be a cheerleader at all."

"It doesn't matter," said Leila. "Coach Steele wants you. And so do I."

From the look on Leila's face, Devin was pretty sure

that all this girl really wanted was a way to take Chloe down. And Devin wanted to stay out of it. "Sorry, Leila. I just don't think it's a good idea for me. And I haven't decided who I am going to vote for yet, if I vote at all." Devin started to walk toward her ceramics class, but turned around after a few steps. "Thanks for warning me, though. About the narc, I mean." Devin somehow felt that she had been warned about more than that, though. If she was going to be a Northside cheerleader, she'd have to stay far away from both Chloe and Leila—and whatever was between them.

CHAPTER 5

"You voted, right?" Chloe asked Kate for the third time. The two girls were hanging out by the front entrance of the school. They still had a solid fifteen minutes before the bell rang for first period. Hundreds of students were beginning to file in from the parking lot. They meandered around, socializing and making last-minute grabs for books from their lockers.

"Of course I did!" Kate reassured her. "Just relax. I'm sure you have nothing to worry about."

Chloe nodded. "I know, sorry. Things have just been so strange lately that I almost wouldn't be surprised if Leila somehow managed to win captain after all. I mean . . . I still can't believe Coach let Devin join the team! Tryouts were so long ago!" Chloe's hazel eyes bugged out as she spoke.

Kate had been hearing this from Chloe all week, so she had a few stock answers to choose from. "Well, it is kind of unfair that she didn't come to camp or anything," Kate admitted. She didn't really like talking about people behind their backs, so she tried her best to remain neutral whenever possible. "But you have to admit that she's pretty good for a newcomer."

"Maybe her tumbling is, but everything else needs major work," Chloe replied huffily. "I could barely hear her voice when we were going over cheers yesterday."

"She'll get it," Kate reassured her. "Don't worry, she's not here to ruin anything. I'm sure she wants to win Regionals just as much as we all do."

"Let's hope so," said Chloe, scanning the incoming students for anyone with red hair. As if just looking at Devin would provide some insight into these strange circumstances. But Devin was nowhere to be seen. "I don't want anyone dragging us down—friend of Coach Steele or not."

Emily skipped up to her friends, interrupting their serious chat with her bubbly excitement. "Hey, girls! You look amazing! This is the first day ever that I haven't questioned my outfit choice twice before leaving for school!"

"Me too," said Kate, nibbling on a warm butter croissant from the breakfast cart. The three friends were wearing the exact same thing because it was Friday, and that meant one thing—game day.

"We do look good, huh?" Chloe said, smiling as she smoothed down the thick fabric of her brand-new cheerleading uniform. The custom-made sets fit them perfectly: bold blue shell tops and A-line skirts edged with white-and-gold trim. A loopy cursive NORTHSIDE was emblazoned across their chests. Chloe's blond hair was tied up in a high ponytail, and she'd even gotten up a little early to curl the ends. She felt powerful and confident, like she was finally a real part of this school.

"Emily! Hey, girls!" a burly football player shouted at them as he walked by. A couple of his friends waved, too. Emily couldn't help but feel cool because some seniors had just acknowledged her and her friends, even if one of them was her big brother Chris.

"I mean, I know we're supposed to care about more than the cute uniform, but can I just say that I'm *obsessed* with this uniform?!" Emily did a twirl, almost toppling over with the weight of her backpack and spilling some of her coffee on the ground. The trim on her skirt sparkled in the morning sunlight as she spun.

"Whoa, watch it, Em!" Kate hopped away. "I don't want to spend my first game of the season covered in coffee stains. There's got to be a demerit for that. Is there a demerit for that?" Kate straightened her top, as if she were being judged at this very moment. Her eyes searched the halls, presumably looking for Coach Steele.

Emily giggled. "Sorry, dude! I'm just so pumped. But this *is* my second cup and it's only seven twenty-one, so maybe I do need to chill out on the caffeine," she said as she took another huge gulp of latte from her NHS ATHLETICS BOOSTERS travel mug. The letters were faded and chipping off. It had been at the Arellano family's house for years— ever since Emily's oldest brother, Eddie, had played on the football team ten years ago. Her parents were NHS superfans.

"Please do—we really don't need another Emily-and-sugar situation on our hands," Chloe added, referring to the second day at camp when Emily drank too many sugary drinks and had to sit down during an entire stunting class because she was actually *too* amped up. "Just water. Tons of water."

"This is totally my last one," Emily said, her eye twitching a little.

Another group of older guys walked past them, all sporting shaggy haircuts and vintage T-shirts. One of them had on a letter jacket that said TRACK & FIELD. Chloe held her breath as he turned around for a double take. He smiled at her and whispered something to his equally attractive friend. Chloe realized she wasn't the only one who'd noticed the guys, though. Emily's expression was one she usually reserved for an Oreo milk shake at Diggy's Diner.

"I feel like I'm famous or something," Emily said, marveling at her surroundings and the students who kept glancing their way.

"Everyone is staring at us. So I'd say we sort of are now," said Chloe. "At least at Northside."

Kate sifted through her backpack, mumbling something about flash cards. It was hard to say if she was actually looking for something or if her shyness had gotten the better of her again. It always amused Chloe and Emily that Kate could be so fearless on the field or the competition floor, and such a wimp when it came to things like making small talk with a classmate or eye contact with a boy she liked.

"Oh, look, fresh cheerleaders," a short guy with a wrestler's build said to his buddy as they passed the group. Emily waved.

"Nope. Not happening. Let's go," Chloe said, grabbing Emily and Kate and steering them down the main hallway toward their first-period classes. None of them needed a guy right now. Chloe had already spent a ton of energy the past week successfully avoiding her middle school crush, Greg Marina. She needed to focus on securing captain. Not on the way that Greg's eyes got cute little crinkles around them when he smiled.

"Whoa, Chloe. What's the rush? What just happened?" Emily said as they quickly wove through the crowd, making a beeline for the language wing.

"Just a G.M. Alert," Chloe lied. Her friends would accept that excuse more readily than a new overarching "no boys" rule.

"You can't avoid him forever, you know," Emily said, looking over her shoulder. She didn't see Greg anywhere behind them. "Just because you told him at the eighth-grade dance that you liked him and he responded by saying 'cool' and then dancing with Leila all night does not mean you have to dash into the nearest corner every time you see him."

"Actually, yes, it does," Chloe said, trying to calm herself. This was a new year and a new, much larger school. The two of them could totally coexist and never have to talk to each other. That was realistic, right?

"Oh, hey, Chloe!"

Chloe whipped around and found herself face-to-face with none other than Greg himself. So much for her earlier excuse. "Hi, Greg," she replied casually, casting her eyes down to the dirty hallway linoleum. She didn't want to look at him if she didn't have to. The sight of him still made her a little weak, even after his rejection. She tried to focus on her new cheerleading shoes instead, which were bright white, sparkling clean, and beautiful. "What's up?"

Greg was tall. The kind of tall you hated to find yourself behind at a concert. He had short, messy brown hair that was always noticeably lighter in September than it was in May and a lean physique sculpted by surfing and beach volleyball. It was true that he was cute. But it was also true that he had gone out with Leila, and that made him much less desirable.

"Wow, you look great in your new uniform." He smirked as his eyes scanned her. Chloe knew that she should have just said hi and kept walking, but she was completely immobilized now. Within a few short moments, the conversation had started to create a traffic jam of students. The halls were crowded as it was, but Greg stood right in the middle of the walkway, making people angry. Everyone was still in that phase of trying to get to class on time to make a good impression on their teachers. Come October it would be a different story.

"What's the holdup?" Leila asked loudly. "Some of us have places to be, Davis." She poked her head around and saw Greg. "Oh, I didn't see you there, Greg," Leila said, her voice immediately climbing in pitch and taking on a sickly-sweet quality. She made no effort to avoid brushing against him as she squeezed past. "Text me later?" Leila said with a sly smile.

Emily rolled her eyes. Time was running out before the bell rang. And cheerleaders did not get tardy slips.

"Well, Greggo Waffles, this has been a super-interesting chat and so, *so* much fun, but we really have to get going. Like, *now*," Emily said with a wave, pulling on Chloe's arm.

For once Chloe was thankful to be rescued by Emily's brashness. Emily put her arm around Chloe like a celebrity security guard and gently forced her down the hall.

"Do you think he looked good?" Chloe asked. "He looked really good...."

Emily ignored Chloe's dreamy tone and turned to say good-bye to Kate as she split off down a connecting corridor. "See you later, Kater!" she yelled.

Even after Kate had lost sight of her friends' blue-and-gold uniforms, she could still hear Emily's lightning-fast chatter as she tried to distract Chloe from the run-in with Greg. *That girl really does need to lay off the caffeine*, Kate thought as she walked through the door of Advanced English. It was only five days into the school year, but this was already her favorite place to be, other than cheerleading practice.

Kate slid into her seat and pulled out her blue English binder. She'd been using blue for her English classes ever since elementary school. Any other color just felt wrong. Blue seemed like good luck, especially now that she was an NHS cheerleader, and it served her well today as she had barely made it to class before the first bell rang. Kate let out a deep breath. That was cutting it way too close. Next time, she'd be at her desk a full ten minutes before class started so she'd have time to look over her notes.

Kate was just flipping through her highlighted copy of *The Scarlet Letter*, thinking about how weird it was for the letter *A* to have a negative connotation, when a deep voice suddenly interrupted her train of thought.

"Wow, a cheerleader, eh? Didn't peg you for the type." It was the boy who sat next to her. *Adam*, she remembered from her teacher taking roll call on the first day. He had black hair and was wearing horn-rimmed glasses that somehow managed to look both seriously nerdy and incredibly cool. Today his shirt had a picture of a sad T. rex trying to play basketball. It was actually sort of funny—the poor dinosaur was trying to slam-dunk and failing because of his teeny-tiny arms.

A few moments passed before she mustered the courage to respond. How did this random junior think he knew her "type"? "Excuse me?" she answered quietly. "What's that supposed to mean?"

"Hey, don't get offended. But that"—he pointed to her massive, bulging backpack—"is not a cheerleader's bag."

"Why not?" she asked. Now she actually was starting to take offense. He had just basically told her that her bag was ugly.

"I'm just surprised, is all. Most Northside cheerleaders don't carry around *Anna Karenina* and all of their textbooks." His smile was genuine. He leaned over to her desk and dropped his voice to a whisper. "It's not a bad thing, Cheer Girl. I think it's pretty awesome that you love school. It's like you're one of us—you're a secret geek. I'm Adam Findlay, by the way."

Kate fought hard not to smirk. As cute as he was, she couldn't let him get away with stereotyping her friends and teammates. "Thanks, Adam Findlay, but I think you have the wrong idea about cheerleaders. You might want to educate yourself a little more before you speak next time." Kate was surprised at her own sass. Maybe hanging out with Emily so much was starting to rub off on her.

Adam leaned back in his desk and looked at Kate in a way she'd never seen before. It was like she was the *New York Times* crossword and he was trying to solve her.

Twenty minutes later, during a class discussion on the previous night's reading, Mrs. Lawrence called on Kate before she'd even had a chance to raise her hand. Kate had already solidified her reputation as an overachiever. "Ms. MacDonald, do you think *The Scarlet Letter* has any relevance in modern society?"

Kate realized this was the perfect opportunity to drive home her point about snap judgments. She cleared her throat and gathered her courage. "Yes, I do. Hester Prynne was a woman under public scrutiny—completely misunderstood and ultimately judged by everyone because of something she had to wear. People, including Hester, are not always what they appear to be. Even in modern-day high school." When she finished talking, Kate sneaked a sideways glance at Adam. Rather than looking defeated, though, he looked impressed. Whether she liked it or not, it appeared Kate MacDonald had just recruited a new fan.

CHAPTER 6

"I've been focusing so much on learning the cheers and routines that I completely forgot about the fact that we'd get to stare at the football team for the whole night!" Emily sprang up and down like a giddy little kid as she spoke, her ponytail swinging wildly. It was unclear whether she was trying to warm up her muscles or she was just overly excited about game night.

"I know. Did you see Dean Stratford in his uniform?" Kalyn Min asked, jogging up to join the group. She lifted her arms high above her head in a stretch and then started to swing them around aggressively. Warm-up chat probably looked a little silly to anyone watching.

"Um, yes. I even went to talk to my brother as the team was leaving the locker room so I could snag the first peek," Emily admitted, giggling.

"Can you guys please try to keep your hormones in check for one night?" Chloe snapped. She was in serious game mode now. Kalyn looked embarrassed and a little hurt. "Sorry. I just mean we should all be warming up and focusing for the game. Boy talk later, okay?" Chloe added cheerfully. She didn't want to sound like a downer and ruin everyone's fun.

"Lighten up, Chloe! Everything is going to be great," Kate assured her. We've been practicing our butts off."

"Ain't that the truth?" Emily reached for a high five. "I can't even see your butt anymore, Kate! Where is that thing?"

Chloe laughed. "You guys are crazy. Now come on, let's stretch!"

Chloe bent down to touch her toes and when she rose back up, there was Devin, the newest obstacle in her path to glory. Chloe had always thought she had it rough with Leila around, whining and making rude comments, but Devin was a different story. Everyone actually seemed to like Devin, and she'd finally started to prove herself in practice toward the end of the week. Chloe tried to remind herself that it was a good thing. Having a weak new squad member would have been way worse. *Let's see how well she remembers the cheers tonight,* Chloe thought. There was no way Devin wasn't going to choke at least once.

"Hey, Devin, glad to see the uniform fits! You look great, girl!" Carley raved.

"Yeah, it was so lucky that Coach Steele was able to track down Raina's old one for you," Jenn added. Raina Delaney had left the JV squad midseason last year to focus on her track-and-field career.

"Thanks, guys," Devin replied, still feeling a little awkward in her new role as cheerleader. But the school colors really did complement her red hair nicely, and she was wearing a special wolf-paw temporary tattoo on her cheek, like the rest of the squad.

Chloe continued with her stretch routine, and a few of the other girls, including Emily and Kate, followed suit. "Devin, do you want to join us?" Chloe asked, hoping to establish herself as the one who would be inviting Devin to do things, not the other way around.

Devin lit up. It was the first time Chloe had really extended the hand of friendship.

"Yeah, that'd be great!"

Now that Devin had joined in, practically everyone on the team was following Chloe's lead. The only holdouts were Leila; her long-standing sidekick, Marcy; and Arianna, Leila's newest recruit from Los Gatos. The three of them had been avoiding Devin all week at practice. Chloe wondered if Leila was just as intimidated by the new girl as she was. In any case, the trio stretched quietly on the sidelines, whispering and laughing wickedly. They were pointing to Carley, who had stopped stretching for a moment and was trying to discreetly pick a wedgie.

"Hey, Carley!" Leila shouted at her. "Hasn't anyone ever told you to lay off the crack?"

"Hey, Leila!" Emily shouted back. "Why don't you stop staring at our butts and get off yours?" Everyone started laughing, and Leila made a face resembling someone who'd sucked on a lemon.

The stands looked almost full. It was a great showing for the JV game, which always drew a smaller crowd than the Varsity one later in the evening. In the stands, Chloe could make out the parents of several of the girls on the squad, all wearing blue-and-gold sweatshirts and visors. There was something magical about the football field during a game night. The bright lights illuminating the massive green expanse, the sound of the PA system announcing the player lineup, and the marching band playing the NHS fight song to amp up the blue-and-gold-clad Timberwolves fans. It just felt like fall. No matter what happened tonight, this energy was what Chloe truly loved about being a cheerleader.

Nonetheless, she still couldn't help feeling that the outcome of tonight's announcement would shape the rest of her life. If she made JV captain, she was likely to do the same on the Varsity team, and then who knew where that would take her in college. She could almost see her beautiful future unfurling like a red carpet in front of her. She visualized Coach Steele announcing her name, followed by the proud looks on her parents' faces as they realized that their youngest daughter had the same extraordinary talent and leadership abilities as the rest of their family.

Visualization, which her dad had taught her, was a great strategy for achieving great things. Whenever Chloe landed a jump or a tumbling pass perfectly, she had first pictured it in her head. If she made captain, she was going to make sure the rest of the squad used the same technique. As her dad said, the brain was a powerful thing.

"Chlo!" her dad shouted as he walked up the steps, looking for some empty seats in the bleachers. Paul Davis still had on his gray suit from working at the law firm all day. Chloe wished he was wearing team colors, but was happy to see that he'd at least thought to bring an old NHS foam finger from the Jake-and-Clementine days. Her mom, Joanie Davis, was probably still working and would turn up before halftime. Thank goodness there was no sign of Greg. She was still reeling from their run-in in the hallway earlier and did not need any more distractions, like attractive ex-crushes, throwing her off.

The band started playing, signaling that the game was

about to begin. Chloe did a couple of quick jumps to shake out her nerves and then locked eyes with Coach Steele, whose expression seemed to say *Take the lead*. Chloe nodded and took a deep breath.

"LET'S GO, TIMBERWOLVES!" Chloe shouted at the top of her lungs. The girls took to their formation facing the stands. The squad stood tall, bodies perfectly straight and hands clasped tight.

"LET'S GO, TIMBERWOLVES!" the squad repeated. Then they clapped twice and raised their arms into a high V.

"LET'S GO, TIMBERWOLVES!" *Clap, clap.* "LET'S GO, TIMBERWOLVES!" *Clap, clap.*

The sound of eighteen girls shouting in unison was powerful and strong. Everyone in the stands began to clap along and whistle.

"LET'S GO, TIMBERWOLVES!"

Chloe launched herself into a side hurdler—her right leg extended straight out beside her and her left leg bent behind her, parallel to the ground. Every girl in line did the same.

After ten minutes or so of play, the football team called a time-out; it was time for the first cheer of the game! All eyes were on the cheerleaders now that there was a break in the on-field action.

"GO, TIMBERWOLVES, GO!"

"FIRE UP AND SCREAM!"

Everyone clapped in unison, gearing up for the finish.

"YELL N-H-S! N-H-S! N-H-S! N-H-S!"

The squad built extensions together using their brand-new N-H-S signs to get the crowd yelling the school letters. Everyone erupted into a frenzy of hoots and hollers. Chloe, Emily, and Arianna all did kicks and pumped their hands in the air, their index fingers pointing up to indicate "number one." Devin opted for a standing back tuck. And everyone else just jumped and shouted "NHS!" or "GO, WOLVES!"

Chloe looked around at her teammates and the people in the stands. Her dad waved his foam finger, and throngs of students clapped. The JV Timberwolf girls had made their first impression on the fans. Now it was just up to the guys on the football team to bring it home.

Two hours later, things were not looking so rosy for the Wolf Pack. The guys had only scored one field goal, bringing the score to 10–3, and the Medham High Minutemen held the lead. The squad had tried their best to keep up, watching the game intently and choosing the right cheers for the right scenarios. Emily had even contributed by giving Charlie Thompson and Dean Stratford a personal pep talk at halftime, which basically consisted of her flirting with them during the three free minutes she had after the cheerleaders performed their halftime dance routine. Chloe saw Coach Steele narrow her eyes at Emily during that one, not that Emily noticed.

There were only twenty-four seconds left on the clock and little hope left for the team to turn things around. The girls decided to do one more round of "Jump around! Scream and shout! Wolves—spirit is what it's all about!" but the crowd was significantly less enthusiastic than they had been at the start of the game. Chloe was lacking energy, too. Her mind was on the captain announcement, but she tried to cheer as loudly as she could and pump everyone up before the finish. It was hard when the team was so clearly about to lose.

"Ladies! Gather 'round!" Coach Steele called to them, getting up from her NHS folding chair on the side of the track. It was time for one of the famous pep talks Chloe had heard so much about. "Come in close, girls. Huddle up." Everyone formed a circle and crouched down just like they'd seen the players on the field do countless times that night.

"You've lost them," Coach Steele said, glancing directly at Chloe. She combed her fingers through her short bob. It looked more rumpled than usual. "Look at 'em up there."

Chloe took in the sight of the crowd, which had dwindled. The few fans who remained looked bored and uninspired.

"You've been giving it about eighty percent so far, which is only a B. And a low one at that."

Kate frowned at Coach's words.

"Now, Bs are okay—for some other teams. Maybe Breckenridge or Elliot High." Chloe stiffened at the mention of their two biggest rivals. "But Northside? We're an A-plus squad! We *do* the extra credit.... We *log* the hours.... We give one hundred and ten percent, and we get it straight back from our fans, no matter what the scoreboard says! Am I right?" The coach's voice rose.

"YEAH!" half of the girls shouted, nodding their heads.

"I said—AM. I. RIGHT. GIRLS?" Coach was smiling.

"YEAH!" they all shouted, feeling the energy.

"N-H-S!" Chloe chanted.

"N-H-S!" the rest of the squad echoed. "N-H-S! N-H-S!" The cheer spread throughout the stands and lasted until the last buzzer went off. It didn't even matter that they'd lost— they'd stuck with their team till the end. The girls felt proud as they walked over to the benches to gather up their gear and grab bottles of water and Gatorade.

"OMG!" Leila practically shouted to Marcy. "It's finally time for the announcement!" The fans were exiting the bleachers, but the squad hung back, waiting for Coach Steele to talk about the captain vote.

"I'm sorry, but does she think she's getting captain?"

Emily scoffed, trying her best to suppress genuine laughter at the notion.

"Well, Marcy and Arianna probably voted for her," Kate replied after taking a long sip of water. "But she is seriously delusional if she thinks any of the rest of us did."

"Man, I'm so nervous," Chloe squeaked, suddenly shy. Her palms felt really sweaty. "What if I don't get it?"

"Oh, you know—your life will be horrible and you'll never amount to anything," Emily deadpanned.

"That's not funny." Chloe playfully smacked Emily's arm as they headed over to Coach Steele. "You know that's actually my biggest fear, right?"

"Yes—that's what makes you so nuts, but also so insanely awesome," Emily replied.

"I'm going to pretend I only heard the second part of that statement," Chloe said.

"Come on, guys!" Jenn hollered. "We have to hurry 'cause Varsity is starting soon!" A ton of upperclassmen had started to fill the stands, along with different parents and more of the teachers. The Varsity cheer squad had already begun warming up. Chloe admired them from afar. She planned to stay for the Varsity game to watch the squad perform.

Coach Steele's voice brought Chloe's attention back to her own team. "JV Wolves. I have . . . in this envelope . . . the name of your new captain," Coach Steele said, dramatically raising an envelope covered in blue-and-gold stickers high in the air.

What is this—the Oscars? Chloe resisted the urge to grab Kate's hand, the way she'd seen nominees do on TV a million times.

The coach continued. "I have faith that we're going to have a great football season and go on to victory at Regionals. Your captain will be your base. And I want to see this team fly."

Coach Steele ripped open the envelope, and Chloe clenched her jaw tightly. She could see that Leila was doing the same.

"Your new captain is…CHLOE DAVIS!" Coach said with a smile.

Everyone began to clap, and Chloe felt a wave of relief wash over her as she made her way to the front of the group. She'd done it! She was the new captain of the Junior Varsity cheerleading team. Her parents were going to be so proud.

"Woooo!" screamed Emily. "Get it!"

"Go, Chlo!" Kate cheered.

"AND…" Coach Steele continued, reading the paper from the envelope.

"And?" said Chloe, thinking she'd heard wrong.

"…DEVIN ISLE! Give it up for your new JV Timberwolves cocaptains!" The coach clapped as she made this final pronouncement.

Both Devin and Chloe stood frozen in their spots, staring first at Coach Steele, then at each other. This had to be a joke. Or a mistake. Or *something*. There was no way that Devin could also be captain, Chloe thought. The look on Devin's face implied that she would agree.

"The results of the vote are nonnegotiable," Coach Steele said before anyone had the chance to protest. "It's going to be a wonderful season. Great first game, girls!"

CHAPTER 7

The moment she got to her room, Chloe changed out of her uniform and into her pajamas. She needed to think as normal Chloe, not Cheerleader Chloe. If such a difference existed. She removed the paw-print tattoo from her cheek with a piece of tape—an old cheerleader trick that Clementine had taught her—and tried to piece together what exactly had just happened. Was it really possible that a new girl, someone with no previous cheerleading experience, had somehow managed to win a spot as captain alongside her?

Chloe had trained for this for years. Since the moment she attended her first Northside High football game in the fifth grade to watch Clementine cheer, she'd known that one day she would be out there leading the crowd and performing incredible stunts. Devin, on the other hand, had just shown up. She probably didn't even know Northside High existed until a few months ago! And now they had to be partners.

Chloe grabbed her teddy bear, which was wearing a blue-and-white cheerleading uniform and holding miniature poms. She sat down in her swivel desk chair and did a spin before stopping in front of her computer. She logged on and opened a browser to check out a few of her regular sites. There was no way she was getting a jump on any of her weekend homework tonight, anyway. She was too worked up.

After checking out her social media sites, she logged on to the new Tumblr blog she'd recently created for the JV team. It wasn't like she was going to abandon the project just because she was mad about the whole Devin thing.

Chloe uploaded a picture of Emily, Kate, and herself in their uniforms and wrote a short post about the first game against Medham, emphasizing how hard the team had worked in order to stay positive despite the loss. She begrudgingly added the results of the captain vote to the end of it. *Chloe Davis and Devin Isle—cocaptains.* Seeing the names written out like that made it seem more real. She hovered over the Publish button, but it didn't feel right. She needed a second opinion.

Luckily, Emily appeared in her chat list at that exact moment.

> **TimberChloeD:** emmmm. need ur help.
> **ShinyEmily:** whoa, u ok? that was intense!
> **ShinyEmily:** thought u were going to faint when coach told everyl
> **TimberChloeD:** yeah, I'm just so confused, u kno?
> **ShinyEmily:** well it is crazay
> **ShinyEmily:** but honestly I'm not that surprised
> **TimberChloeD:** u aren't?
> **TimberChloeD:** u knew Devin was going to get it too?
> **ShinyEmily:** no, but u have to admit— girl's got skillz
> **ShinyEmily:** she's been helping a lot of ppl on their tumbling stuff

Chloe couldn't believe Emily was taking Devin's side. Had Devin really been helping the other girls so much that the vote was tied? Or was this a Coach Steele call? Either way, Emily was supposed to be her best friend, and that meant not sticking up for Devin.

TimberChloeD: r u trying to say u think she should be cocaptain?

ShinyEmily: no! just sayin it might not be so bad. someone to share the work!

ShinyEmily: wish I had that. I just signed up for student council and dance committee for homecoming. hoping to get travis hollister's band to perform...now who's the crazy one?

TimberChloeD: that's awesome, em. maybe they will let u sing with them

ShinyEmily: u know me so well ;)

TimberChloeD: well i'm wiped. going 2 bed. can't handle this devin stuff right now...

ShinyEmily: hey chlo—we are all a team, remember?

TimberChloeD: course. go wolves!

Emily signed off and Chloe realized she had never even asked her to read over the blog entry. She hit Publish anyway and shut down her computer. It didn't matter. She doubted anyone would even look at it.

As she lay in bed trying to fall asleep, Chloe wondered where her visualizations had gone wrong. Nowhere in any of them had there been an extra captain with whom she had to share all the glory and the responsibility. The concept had never even occurred to her as a possibility. But that was the thing about cheerleading—you never knew what sort of new, amazing feat you were going to have to pull off while keeping a smile plastered on your face. *Mind over matter*, Chloe thought as she closed her eyes.

CHAPTER 8

When Devin woke up the next morning, she tried to recall the events of the previous night at the game. The way she'd worn the blue-and-gold uniform and pulled her hair up into a high ponytail topped with a white bow, just like a little clone of Sage, albeit in different school colors. The strange feeling of shouting cheers up at the stands, when she'd spent so many years as the one looking down at the field. And, finally, the unexpected announcement that she was cocaptain of the team, much to Chloe Davis's obvious dismay.

None of it seemed real, so maybe it was just an odd dream. But the Northside uniform hung on the back of her door, freshly washed since last night (thanks to her mom's borderline obsessive-compulsive tendencies). Emerald hopped up onto the bed, turned around in a little circle, and nestled into the covers. "Where are we, Emmy?" Devin asked the cat, but her response was just a louder purr. "And what the heck am I doing with all of this cheerleading stuff?"

Devin turned on her laptop and was just logging on when she heard voices and laughter coming from the kitchen. For a moment Devin wondered what sort of visitor they would have on a Saturday morning. Then it hit her... Sage! Devin really needed to see her sister. She rushed down the hallway, not even bothering to throw on her sweatpants.

"Good morning, Devin!" Coach Steele chirped, cradling a steaming cup of coffee in an old Spring Park General Hospital mug. She sat at the green Formica table across from Linda, who was smiling and nibbling on a pastry.

"Oh, I thought..." Devin said, trying to hide her disappointment that it wasn't her big sister after all. She pulled her large T-shirt down to cover herself more.

Linda got up from the table and walked to the cupboard. "Did we wake you, honey? Sorry—Meg and I just got to talking, and we were remembering that time at the Spring Park Cheerleading Crab Feed fund-raiser when you ate that clam chowder and thought it was chicken."

Devin cringed. She knew the story well.

"And then what did she say again?" Coach Steele laughed.

"I believe it was . . . 'Mom, why is this chicken so chewy?' " Linda recalled.

"Oh, Dev, it was priceless—the look on your face when we told you," Coach Steele continued. "You really didn't want to think about eating clams."

"But then again, you were only nine," Linda added, shaking her head at the happy memory.

"I still hate clam chowder," said Devin as she walked into the family room, grabbing a pair of shorts from a pile of unfolded laundry on the sofa. "Some things never change."

"But some doooo!" Linda said in a singsong as she made Devin a cup of tea. "Like the fact that now *both* my girls are star cheerleaders."

"Were," Devin said, returning to the kitchen and sitting down at the table. "Both of us *were* cheerleaders. I'm actually glad you're here, Coach. I don't know if I can do this. Cocaptain? I mean . . ."

Coach Steele's expression remained unchanged. "I thought you might say that. Which is exactly why I wanted to pay you guys a visit this morning."

"I've pretty much made up my mind, Coach," Devin replied, shrugging. "I'm really not cut out for cheerleading. Did you see me on that field? I was trying, but it was a disaster. And the other girls clearly don't want me there. I don't know why you decided to make me a captain." She began to twirl one of her curls around her finger.

"Are you crazy, Devin?" Coach Steele said. "I would never impose captain on you. No offense, of course. But you're brand-new!" Coach scoffed. "How would that be fair?"

"So what are you saying?" Devin asked.

Linda chimed in. "She's saying, Dev, that those girls elected you because they believe in your talents. Isn't that right, Meg?"

"More or less," Coach Steele admitted. She took a long sip of coffee and stared at Devin. "Trust me—I know you're talented. I've always wanted you on one of my teams. But I was surprised, too, when I saw how many of the girls wanted you to lead them. I thought they'd all go for Chloe Davis. But you actually got one more vote than she did. You must have made quite an impression this week, kid."

"I did?" Devin felt flattered and then suddenly remembered her weird conversation with Leila at lunch the other day. It was impossible to ignore. She should probably tell Coach Steele about it now. What if the vote had been a sham—designed by Leila to take down an old rival? Devin couldn't feel good about that.

Linda put the mug of steaming tea down in front of Devin, along with a toasted poppy seed bagel. "Look, Dev, Meg brought us breakfast goodies."

The words spilled out of Devin's mouth. "I think Leila

Savett rigged the vote," she confessed. She twirled the curl around her finger a little bit tighter.

"What makes you think that?" Coach Steele wrinkled her forehead in concern. "There's really no way Leila could have cheated. I received individual e-mails from each of the girls on the squad."

"Well, she told me she wanted to make me captain," Devin said. "I know this has something to do with her—"

"Devin, that's ridiculous!" Linda said, sitting down at the table with them. She turned to Coach Steele. "Meg, please talk some sense into her."

Coach Steele stood up from the table and smiled. "Devin, whether you want to believe it or not, your peers like you. And I believe in you. I won't let you quit now. I'll see you at practice on Monday."

As soon as she saw Coach Steele's silver SUV pull out of the driveway, Devin started to chew on her bagel. She considered the option that maybe she had actually been chosen for the role by the others. It made her feel special, but she couldn't shake the idea that it was all a lie. Chloe Davis deserved it so much more. It was only right for Devin to step down from the team.

"I still don't know, Mom," Devin whined. "I don't think I can take all the drama."

"Honey, it would mean so much to me if you kept with it," Linda implored. "Just until Christmas break?"

Devin sighed and propped her chin on one hand.

Linda reached out and squeezed her daughter's other hand. "Hey, what would you say to me flying Josh down here for New Year's?"

Devin squealed. She leaped up and hugged her mom. "Yes! Yes! Oh, thank you!"

"So you'll stay on the team, then?"

"Yes! Whatever you want!" Devin exclaimed. She didn't even care that it was technically a bribe.

CHAPTER 9

Chloe already made a point to arrive early to practice every day, but she thought that if she went straight from last period to the gym after school, she might be able to catch Coach Steele alone to find out how the cocaptain decision had been reached. It was, after all, a combination of peer votes and Coach Steele's opinion that determined who landed the position. But she wanted—no, needed—to know the factors involved, for the sake of her own sanity. Chloe hadn't been sleeping well since the announcement was made.

"Someone's got somewhere important to be!" Mr. Reaser joked in last-period algebra. Chloe had been staring at the clock for the last ten minutes of class, eagerly waiting for the bell to ring. When it finally did, she ran out of the classroom, grabbed her duffel from her locker, and sprinted to the changing room. But when Chloe arrived there, she realized that she wasn't alone.

"Hey, Devin," Chloe said, trying her best to hide her disappointment. *This girl is always on my heels, or one step ahead in this case*, Chloe thought. "What's going on?"

"Just wanted to try some things on the mats before practice." Devin shrugged. "Tumbling kind of Zens me out, you know?"

Actually, Chloe did know. "Yeah, the way you have to completely trust yourself and you can't really hesitate. Otherwise you could get hurt," Chloe said as she took out her cheerleading clothes. "It's as much a mental exercise as it is a physical one."

"Totally!" Devin's eyes widened. "Have you ever done gymnastics?"

"Me? No way. Strictly cheerleading. Though I did go to an all-star cheer gym for a couple of years before I had a school team to cheer for." Chloe never liked to mention it to other squad members. It made her feel like she was trying to one-up them by saying she had more training. "Actually, Leila trained there with me."

Devin looked surprised. "You guys have been cheerleading together for that long and you still don't get along?" she asked, genuinely perplexed.

Chloe laughed. "Yeah, well. Don't know if you've noticed, but Leila sort of hates everything. I'm not even sure why she wants to be on the team anymore."

"Yeah, what's the point if you can't get along with your teammates, right?" Devin said, tying one of her new cheer shoes.

Chloe wasn't sure if that statement was supposed to be directed at her or not, but the way Devin said it stung a little.

"Well, I'm heading inside—see you in a few," Devin suddenly said, and she was off.

Is Devin mad? Chloe wondered. *Does she even have a right to be mad?* A few minutes ago, before their conversation, Chloe had thought Devin was nothing more than some girl who'd waltzed into town and been handed a spot on the squad. Now she wasn't so sure.

Chloe had to admit that Devin was trying really hard. She had learned all of the cheers in record time and was now even showing up early to practice her tumbling. Maybe Chloe had underestimated the new girl's commitment to the team.

Chloe jogged out of the locker room and waited by the side entrance to the gym. She'd seen Coach Steele enter from there on most days, and figured it was probably a good spot to catch her.

The Northside High School campus was large and sprawling. Several of the corridors were outdoors, with awnings to provide shade from the harsh California sun. There were four one-story buildings, housing the science, language, math, and elective wings, along with all of the students' lockers. Though the school was relatively new, the blue-and-white paint that covered the sides of the gym and corridors was bleached and chipped from the heavy sun exposure, making everything look as if it had been put through an Instagram filter.

Chloe observed the daily afternoon transition of the school from an institution of academia to a sports complex. Kids wearing various NHS uniforms and toting athletic gear walked between the buildings, rushing to get to their extra-curricular activities. The sun was beating down, even though it was mid-September. Chloe felt beads of sweat forming on her forehead. It didn't matter, though. She would be sweating twenty times as much in the next few hours.

There was a low brick barrier by the side of the gym that looked inviting. Chloe jumped up on it and sat down, stretching her legs out in front of her along the wall and leaning against the building. She closed her eyes momentarily and just listened. She tried to zone out and focus on the birds in the trees.

"Chloe?" Coach Steele shook her. "What are you doing up there?"

"Huh?" Chloe rubbed her eyes, blinking herself awake. "Omigod, I fell asleep!"

"Yes, you did." Coach Steele laughed. "I was a little jealous, actually."

Coach reached out a hand to help Chloe down from her post. Chloe landed with a *thud*. "Ouch." Her little nap had made her body stiff. She needed more rest than she'd been getting lately. Last night she'd tossed and turned—dreaming that everyone at school forgot her name and that Devin started dating Greg.

Coach Steele furrowed her brow. "What's up, Chloe? You're acting very non-Davis right now." She put a hand on her hip and tilted her head slightly to one side, concerned. "If something's wrong, I want to know about it. I really don't want my new JV captain holding back."

Cocaptain, you mean, Chloe thought. "Really? I can bring up anything?" she asked.

"Go for it!"

Chloe took a breath and hesitated. "I guess I'm just curious about why there are two captains instead of one this season." It was wise to choose her words carefully. Devin was obviously Coach Steele's girl, after all. They'd known each other forever, and Chloe didn't want to make it seem as if she didn't like Devin. It was a tricky situation.

"Ah, yes." Coach Steele nodded like she had been completely expecting this conversation all along. "Chloe, you have nothing to worry about. I think you'll find that you and Devin are quite similar, but also very different in ways that will prove really valuable for the squad. I know it's not what you were expecting, but it's both of your jobs now to rise to this challenge together."

Chloe took in Coach Steele's words, looking to the gym door as if it would spell out some sort of answer.

"Your squad needs you," Coach Steele continued. "They all really trust and believe in you." She put her arm around Chloe, leading her into the gym. "Now wake up, girl! We need you alive and kicking to run this practice."

They had walked in just in time to see Devin launch herself into a tumbling pass of Olympic proportions. "Oh, don't worry, I'm definitely awake now," Chloe replied, starting to feel the blood pumping through her veins. Oddly enough, the pep talk had left her feeling even more competitive with Devin than before. Coach Steele had completely glossed over Chloe's question, and it didn't sit right.

Chloe jogged over to the mat and started doing some laps around Devin. Coach Steele called out to them, "I just have to stop by the office to do some paperwork. You girls okay?"

"Yeah, Coach," Chloe hollered back. "We're good!"

Practice wasn't due to start for another twenty minutes, but why not get in some extra tumbling? She could almost match Devin in skill level, and that was without the years of formal gymnastics training.

"Want to throw some passes together?" Chloe asked Devin, whose face was flushed red from activity. She was breathing hard and had a bead of sweat running down her forehead.

"Yeah! Of course!" Devin responded eagerly. "Maybe I could show you some of the stuff I wanted to put in our competition routine?"

So she'd been choreographing their routine already. Interesting.

"Let's see, then," Chloe challenged. She took a place in the corner of the mat, stretching in a standing straddle position. Devin may not have known it, but Chloe could feel that this was about to be a showdown.

"I thought it might be cool to do a round-off, two back handsprings, layout. Like this." Devin ran to the edge of the mat, took a breath, and sprang forward. Her form was perfect, Chloe begrudgingly thought.

"That looks great and all when you do it, but I know this squad better than you do. I know each and every one of their strengths and weaknesses," Chloe said as she walked over to where Devin had started the combination. "And I know that only three of them can do that."

"Then we can teach the rest of them." Devin failed to

see a flaw in her plan. "Why only try the easy stuff? That's so lame."

"Because people get hurt when they attempt things they aren't ready for," Chloe said, an edge to her voice. "It's better to stick to things everyone can do, and do them well."

Chloe prepped for a pass. "Watch and learn."

She took off, jumping into a clean single round-off back handspring. It was simple, but definitely something the entire squad could pull off. "See? Keep it clean and everyone stays together. As a team."

"I disagree. The only squads who win are the ones who push themselves toward greatness by taking risks." Devin heard herself speak the words, but she almost couldn't believe they'd come out of her mouth. She sounded exactly like Sage.

"Tumbling only counts for ten points of the final score at competition. The judges also score on the execution and difficulty of jumps, pyramids, and dance. We can't spend all our time trying to work on a few tumbling passes because they're the only thing you know how to do," Chloe said as she strutted over to Devin, hands on hips. "You know, watching your older sister perform on her squad does *not* count as cheerleading experience. I did plenty of that, too. It wasn't until I actually got on the mats myself that I knew what it was to be a cheerleader."

"Look, I didn't ask for any of this," Devin countered. "And I'm only trying to help make the team better!"

"The team was fine before you came along," Chloe responded.

"Whoa, you guys," Emily said, stepping between the bickering cocaptains. Devin's face fell and Chloe immediately grew silent, realizing that half the squad had entered the gym and seen their little display of unsportsmanship. Leila stood in the corner smiling, as if to say *I knew you couldn't handle being captain.*

Chloe was beyond embarrassed. This wasn't her.

Devin looked down at the mats in shame. Who had she become?

The JV Timberwolves had some serious work to do.

CHAPTER 10

All forty Junior Varsity and Varsity cheerleaders sat on the stage of the auditorium. They wore their uniforms and attempted to look peppy, even though it was only 7:00 AM. Coach Steele stood facing them, her back to the audience seats. She had on her normal game-day outfit— blue-and-gold Northside High warm-ups, trimmed with the same striping as their uniforms, and her usual running sneakers. Other coaches often just wore jeans and a school T-shirt to games, but Coach Steele took pride in matching her girls. If they dressed up to show their spirit, why wouldn't she?

"Thanks for meeting me before school today, girls. I know it was last minute, but I just wanted to go over some things before today's game-day pep rally." Coach Steele's voice seemed to be lacking its typical enthusiasm. "And to give you some news. But first—"

"What sort of news?" one of the Varsity girls shouted.

"Spill it, Coach!" said another.

Apparently, Coach Steele liked to use dramatic buildup in her speeches to the Varsity squad, too.

Coach Steele cleared her throat and ran her fingers through her messy hair. "Well, I don't want to put too much pressure on you all, but I think you deserve to know."

Chloe began to feel nervous. Good news never started with a sentence like that. She looked over at Devin and wondered if she already knew whatever the announcement was, being friends with the coach and all. But Devin's face was blank.

Coach Steele began to pace back and forth. "I met with Principal Cilento yesterday. Budget meetings are coming up, and we really need to prove ourselves in order to keep our funding."

"What does that mean?" asked Jenn.

"The school Athletics Boosters club can't afford to keep sending such a large team to competitions unless we are a champion squad again. The funds have to go to the other teams."

A million conversations erupted at once, and several hands shot into the air.

"Calm down, ladies! You can put your hands down because I'm not going to answer any of your questions," Coach Steele said, shaking her head. "And you know why? Because we are not going to lose at Regionals! I believe in each and every one of you. In all my years of coaching, I have never seen such a talented group of cheerleaders." Coach Steele actually looked like she was getting a little teary. "Which is exactly what I told the principal. He agreed."

Chloe remembered the euphoria that had followed when the NHS team had won during Jake's senior year. All this time she had wanted to win purely for that feeling, but now this new information made winning much more important.

Before even thinking about it, Chloe popped up from the floor and began clapping her hands together. "N-H-S! N-H-S!" Chloe shouted, and soon all forty girls had joined in. Coach Steele smiled wide, surveying her teams and their spirit. After a round of "Timber, Timber, Timberwolves!" the girls finally settled down enough to go over the rally plans for later.

As Coach Steele reviewed the schedule, Chloe beamed with enthusiasm and excitement. The group moment had been such a rush that she almost wondered if there really had been a meeting with the principal or if their coach had concocted the whole thing as inspiration for her squads to succeed.

❀

"Let's hear it, freshmen!" Mallory Steiner, the tall, blond Varsity team captain hollered into a microphone at the beginning of the pep rally later that day. She stood in the center of the basketball court, the rest of the squad behind her holding up fight signs and megaphones. Bunches of blue and gold balloons lined the bleachers. "FRESH-MEN! FRESHMEN! FRESHMEN!" the kids sitting in the freshman section chanted.

The JV girls jumped up and down, motioning for their class to get louder. Chloe did a toe touch and pumped her fist into the air. "Go, freshmen!" Jenn and Lexi coordinated a pass involving a back handspring. The crowd went wild.

"All right, all right!" Mallory said into the mic. "Good effort, but I think we have some other Northside fans here that can do even BETTERRRRR! Let's hear it, sophomores!" The next section of bleachers began to chant for their class, trying to be even louder than the freshmen. Next, the juniors had their turn. Each class was louder than the last. When it was finally the seniors' turn, the sounds coming from the gym were so loud the teachers were covering their ears.

"That was great!" Mallory yelled to the crowd. "Please

hold tight while the judges tabulate the scores." The theme from *Jeopardy!* played over the sound system, cued by a girl from Student Council. Mallory did a little dance, swaying back and forth to the music. Finally, a girl from the Varsity team jogged out to Mallory and handed her a piece of poster board folded in half.

"And the winner...of the...CLASS YELL...is..." Mallory covered the microphone and waited for the room to be quiet. She flipped the cardboard open and showed it to the crowd. It said JUNIORS-SENIORS in giant blue letters. "IT'S THE JUNIORS AND SENIORS! It's a tie, everyone!"

The senior class booed loudly from their section. A bunch of the football players in the back row stood up and gave a thumbs-down. "What's that?" Mallory put her hand to her ear dramatically. "You want a tiebreaker!" She motioned for the Varsity cheerleaders to form a quick huddle. It was all part of the show. The JV girls jogged over to join them.

Inside the huddle, Mallory pointed at Kate. "MacDonald, right?"

Kate nodded, clearly surprised that the Varsity captain knew her name. "You are going to choose a volunteer from the senior stands, got it?"

"Got it!" Kate replied, smiling. She felt pretty special and also a bit nervous. The seniors were the rowdiest group. She hoped she wouldn't choose the wrong person.

"Taylor!" Mallory shouted at a cute blond girl with the word *seniors* drawn on her cheek in blue eyeliner. "You grab a volunteer from the juniors! Now... BREAK!" The huddle broke apart, and the chosen girls headed off to complete their assigned sides. A loud club beat blared from the speakers.

Mallory spoke into the mic again. "My girls here will be needing two volunteers! Raise those hands high!"

Kate quickly zeroed in on Emily's brother, Chris Arellano, since he was one of the only seniors she knew. She figured he was a safe bet because he was on the football team and fairly popular. Chris was met with the cheers of his classmates as he pumped his hands in the air proudly. He ran down the steps of the bleachers and onto the basketball court. "Thirty-four! Thirty-four! Thirty-four!" his teammates chanted, calling out his player number. Kate also heard a few high-pitched whistles; no doubt Chris was pretty popular with the senior girls, too.

A round of cheers came from the junior section of the bleachers, and Kate looked over to see which unlucky victim Taylor had selected to go up against Chris in the challenge. She nearly fainted from shock when she saw none other than Adam Findlay, the snarky guy from English class. He jogged forward with his hands up high above his head in a victory pose. He looked like a marathon winner crossing the finish line, except he was wearing jeans and a black T-shirt that said THIS IS MY FRIDAY SHIRT, with his trademark horn-rimmed glasses.

Kate suddenly felt her face grow hot. She really hoped he wasn't about to make a huge fool of himself, even if no one was aware that he and Kate knew each other. Mallory motioned for all the girls to form a line behind the two guys. The cheerleaders stood with their right feet extended forward and their arms high up in the air. They used their "spirit fingers"—wiggling their digits back and forth—since they didn't have their poms.

"Okay, everyone—we have our two tiebreaker contestants here! For the juniors..." Mallory said as she put the mic in Adam's face.

"Adam Findlay!" he shouted into the mic. The junior stands cheered.

"And for the seniors..." Mallory said, doing the same to Chris.

"Chris Arellano." Chris spoke calmly and coolly. The senior stands erupted.

Mallory put her arms around the two boys in a flirty way. "Gentlemen, your challenge is...to show us your best CHEERLEADING MOVE!" The two guys immediately started laughing. Adam's face began to turn red, and everyone in the senior stands started to chant Chris's name.

"Looks like we want Chris to go first!" Mallory shouted. "Ready, Chris?"

Chris nodded and launched himself into a pitiful cart-wheel, legs bent. He stood up, triumphant. His peers continued to cheer him on and he took a dainty bow, miming that he was wearing a dress. Everyone laughed.

"Okay, okay. Good job, Chris! Very pretty! Adam— take it away!" Mallory said, and got the crowd chanting his name. Adam paused for a moment, looking like he was going to completely choke. Kate held her breath. "Adam! Adam!" She joined in the chant, hoping it would help. Finally, Adam centered himself, bent forward, and launched his body into a perfect standing back tuck. It almost looked better than Chloe's! The whole gym, even the seniors, broke out in applause. *No way*, thought Kate.

Mallory ran over to Adam, her blond hair trailing behind her. She grabbed his hand and held it high in the air as if she were the referee in a boxing match. Even though the whole student body was cheering for him, he searched the line of cheerleaders till his eyes landed on Kate. He looked straight at her, smiling, and mouthed the words, "What now, Cheer Girl?"

Kate felt like the wind had been knocked out of her. For the first time, she didn't have the answer to a question.

CHAPTER 11

It was nothing but teal, white, and orange everywhere. Huge handmade posters covered in paint and glitter bore phrases like BEWARE THE BULLDOGS! and BRECKENRIDGE IS THE BEST! A giant twisting arch made of orange and teal balloons framed the home team's bleachers, which were already packed. A group of about thirty girls stretched in front of the stands, checking each other's ponytails and touching up their over-the-top sparkly teal eye shadow.

Most of the Northside JV cheerleaders were busy sizing up their competition, but Emily was inspecting the decorations. "Whoa! Where do you think they got those giant-letter balloons?" she asked as they entered the stands of the

Breckenridge High School football field. Emily pointed to a set of massive white balloons across the way that spelled out BRECKENRIDGE above the home team's stands. "I need to order some of those for us!" She took out her phone and tapped it into her to-do-list app.

"How about ordering some of those cute warm-ups while you're at it, too?" Kalyn said, practically salivating at the sight of the Breckenridge cheerleaders. They wore brand-new teal jackets and pants with glittery orange stripes down the side. "Aren't those the ones we wanted from the catalog?" Arianna whimpered. "It's not fair that their school has so much more funding."

"Well, their squad looks enormous." Devin gaped. "They must be double our size!"

"Actually, they only have about seven more girls than we do. A lot of them also train at Sunny Valley All-Stars," Chloe explained. "Not that having more people matters, of course," she added, a little more loudly, for the benefit of the whole team. Big squads had disadvantages, too. The two teams were in the same division, Large Junior Varsity, but there was way more room for little mistakes in the choreography when twenty-five girls were trying to perform in sync instead of just eighteen.

"Maybe we could ask that dude from the rally to join the squad," Lexi joked. "What was his name again? Alex Finnerty?"

"Adam Findlay," Kate said protectively.

"Whoa, okay," Lexi replied. "Sor-ry. You got a thing for him?"

"No! Sorry, Lexi. Didn't mean to snap. I'm just over-whelmed!" Kate motioned to the rival team's stands. "I mean, I can't believe we got so unlucky tonight! Being matched up against Breckenridge is scary enough, without it also being their homecoming game." Kate frowned. "I hope we score some points so we aren't completely shamed."

From the way the season had been going so far, it was pretty obvious that the Northside football team was going to get pulverized tonight. But the old rivalry between Northside and Breckenridge went beyond football. It was also about which cheerleading squad tossed its teammates higher, who could cheer the loudest, and, ultimately, who would come out on top at Regionals in November. Chloe had watched it all before during Clementine and Jake's time, and she also knew some of the Breckenridge girls from the gym.

"Well, I'm not worried," Emily mused, swinging her sagging duffel bag from one shoulder to the other. "It's pretty unlikely that our guys will win anyway, so at least Breckenridge can enjoy a victory on their homecoming."

"You guys—come on!" Chloe pleaded. "That is no way for us to think! We could totally beat them! Where's your

NHS spirit? What happened to the energy we had at the pep rally today?"

As if on cue, the Breckenridge stands erupted in cheers as the Bulldog girls "practiced" a thrilling stunt sequence identical to one the Northside girls had seen the instructors do at the opening demo at camp. It wasn't even something the campers had been taught.

"Look, all I care about is showing up their squad for once," Carley said. Her gold liquid eyeliner was extra-thick tonight, and she was sporting a large pouf in her light brown ponytail. Chloe suspected she was trying to impress a Breckenridge boy. There was no rule against having a boyfriend at a rival school, but most cheerleaders would say it felt unnatural. *At least they should*, Chloe thought.

Jenn Hoffheimer nodded in agreement. "Remember how smug that girl Karen Gelb was when they won the Top Banana at camp? She looked over to gloat at us specifically, even though there were at least twenty other teams there. So annoying."

"Yeah, she was on the Warren Middle School Warriors last year, too. I hate losing to her." Gemma shook her head in disgust. "Well, I hate losing to anyone, really. But she isn't nice about it."

The girls threw down their bags on the benches, and something made a loud clanging noise.

"Sorry, everyone," Emily said, unzipping her monstrosity of a bag. "That was me. I have all these brass candlesticks for the photo background at our homecoming dance. I'm gonna polish 'em up in my spare time." She looked proud of herself.

Kate and Chloe exchanged a confused look. Candlesticks seemed like a random decoration choice, even for Emily.

"So what is the theme, then?" Chloe asked casually, balancing on one leg like a flamingo, stretching out her right quad. She released it and picked up the other leg. *Please don't let it be vampires*, thought Chloe. *Anything but vampires.*

"A Night in Camelot," answered Emily, smiling. "Isn't that brilliant?"

"What?" Arianna asked. "I don't get it."

"You know, like castles and knights and stuff! We even rented this giant inflatable dragon. I'm totally going to try to get the guys in the band to wear chain-mail vests. The lead guitarist's uncle runs the Halloween Superstore."

"Camelot sounds kind of clichéd, if you ask me," Leila said, wrinkling her nose.

"Good thing no one did," Emily deadpanned. "If you wanted to help choose the theme, maybe you should have volunteered for the dance committee, too."

"How do you find the time to do all of this, Emily?" Jenn asked. "Like, seriously, how are you not dead right now?"

"Trust me, I'm close," Emily assured her. "But it will be so worth it when we've won our own homecoming game. All of you will be dancing in the gorgeous, decorated gym, and I'll be onstage singing with Travis Hollister's band, Hashtag."

"That band of hot junior guys?" Jenn replied, her face dreamy. "I talked to the bassist, Alex, at the movies once. He works the concession booth and gave me a free popcorn," Jenn said wistfully. "That counts as a date, right?"

"I dunno, want me to ask him for you?" teased Emily.

"Noooo!" Jenn yelled like she was falling down a bottomless well, as she slid down to the ground in a right side split.

"Only kidding," Emily replied. "But I can totally hook you up with him at the dance if you want." She went over to her bag and took out a plastic bottle of kombucha tea and gulped down half of it in one sip. "Good for the vocal cords," she explained when she saw Chloe raising her eyebrows.

At least Emily was off the energy drinks.

"All this homecoming talk reminds me—we seriously need to work on our new routines," Chloe noted. She always managed to steer the conversation back to cheerleading. "We'll have to do two—one for the pep rally and one for the game. I don't want anyone seeing repeats this year."

Devin knew from all of her years going to Sage's competitions that she didn't mind watching repeat routines if they were strong and had impressive choreography. Still, she kept her mouth shut. Since the fight with Chloe in the gym before practice that one day, she was again considering stepping down from cheerleading altogether. Even if it meant she'd have to give up seeing Josh on New Year's. She loved tumbling and everything, but the team drama was new to her and hard to take. Maybe she wasn't cut out for the school-sports life, just like Josh had said. Maybe she was more of a lone Timberwolf. Most gymnasts were.

But something was preventing Devin from giving up. She couldn't stand to lose one more thing she cared about. Yes, Devin had to admit, she was starting to care about cheerleading. She could tell that she was good at it, maybe even better than Sage. If she stayed on the team, she'd have to find a way to smooth things out with Chloe. And find a way to tell Josh about everything. But that was an entirely different issue. Her chest tightened just thinking about *that* conversation.

Grinning, Chloe shouted to the squad, "Come on, girls! Time to rock!" She was getting pretty excited to cheer tonight. Both of her parents had said they'd come. She searched the stands, but they weren't there yet. Maybe they'd gone home to change into their fan gear this time.

"Everyone huddle up!" Devin shouted. She caught sight

of her mom sitting in the bleachers, a silly smile plastered on her face. Devin wasn't surprised she'd traveled all the way to an away game. Cheering for Devin had given her mom a new hobby outside of work. Or just reignited an old one.

Throughout the game, the JV Timberwolves stood tall on the sidelines of the field, keeping their legs shoulder width apart and their arms behind their backs, holding their new gold metallic pom-pons. Whenever the guys had the ball, the squad lifted their poms up and shook them, letting the strands glitter in the stadium lighting. Every time there was a break in the action, the girls turned around and led the fans in a new cheer.

"Man, I'm losing my voice already!" Carley croaked with a minute left in the second quarter. "Cheering over this crowd is killer."

"It's just because it's their homecoming game," Jenn said, looking across the field at the massive crowd of Bulldogs fans spilling out from the bleachers. Homecoming events did have a tendency to bring out people in droves, but by halftime, the NHS players on the field weren't the only ones who were intimidated by their longtime rivals.

"Or maybe they just have way more fans than us," Leila commented, loudly enough for Chloe to hear. "Their captain is probably awesome."

"Hold up—whose side are you on again?" Emily said, putting her hands on her hips.

"It would also help if their mascot wasn't holding up a huge sign that says NORTHSIDE SUCKS." Lexi pointed to the costumed character, a giant brown bulldog wearing a spiked collar and a football jersey. The back of the jersey read BRUISER. He danced around, waving the sign and every so often flipping it over to reveal an illustration of a dead timberwolf.

"I kind of love that sign in a weird way," Emily said, her voice equal parts puzzled and amused. "It shows some guts. I want us to have more guts! Maybe we should make some posters of dead Tar Heels for when we play Elliot High."

"Yeah, but what's a Tar Heel, anyway?" Kalyn asked. "Like a bigfoot?"

"I think it's something from the Civil War," Kate offered.

"Let's go, girls!" Coach Steele hollered. She blew her whistle. "Enough of the side chatter! Time to show those Bulldogs girls how it's done!"

Everyone snapped to attention and followed Coach's orders, grabbing their signs and running out onto the field. Once they were set in their double-V formation, facing their own stands, Chloe and Devin signaled the start of the routine by locking eyes and nodding to each other:

one....two...three....At least they appeared united to the audience.

A hush fell over the crowd.

"ALL RIGHT!" Chloe and Devin shouted, their voices echoing out.

Then the rest joined in, stepping forward and raising their right fists high in the air.

"NORTHSIDE FANS...IN THE STANDS. YELL BLUE...AND GOLD!" They pumped their arms in unison and twisted to the side. *Clap. Clap.*

"YELL BLUE AND GOLD!" They pumped their arms to the other side. *Clap. Clap.*

"COME ON, FANS, GET ON YOUR FEET!" Their white smiles could be seen from the very back of the stands as they shouted the words.

"LISTEN TO...THE NORTHSIDE BEAT!"

The girls clapped their hands once more, making sure to keep their lines clean and their arms tight. All of them were on point, even though they hadn't even made it to the stunt portion yet. In practices, the routine had been shaky at best. *Here goes nothing*, Chloe thought as she felt the intimidating JV Bulldogs girls' eyes bearing down on her.

"WE SAY BLUE, YOU SAY GOLD!" they instructed the fans as they walked to their stunt groups. Chloe took her place as a main base, heading to the front of the middle group to prepare to hoist Emily above their heads. Up front, Arianna and Devin held up the large signs that spelled out the school colors.

"BLUE!" Arianna reached her sign up.

A few weak responses of "Gold!" could be heard from the stands.

"BLUE!"

"Gold!" Linda Isle and the Arellano family shouted back, along with some of the teachers.

"WE SAY WOLF PACK, YOU SAY FIGHT!"

Three groups of bases formed and launched their top girls into liberties. They stood high in the air, legs locked and arms up. Luckily, this impressed the crowd enough to make them respond louder this time.

"WOLF PACK!" the cheerleaders yelled, holding the position, top girls stretched up high.

"Fight!" the NHS crowd yelled back.

"WOLF PACK!" The stunt groups released the girls, catching them in cradles.

"Fight!" Arianna and Devin shouted with the crowd up front.

"NORTHSIDE, FIGHT! WOLF PACK, GROWL!"

"OUR MIGHTY WOLF PACK'S ON THE PROWL!"

The eighteen girls froze in formation, awaiting their music cue before starting their dance routine to a remix of "Party Rock Anthem" and "We Found Love." They were already riding high on the wave of doing the "libs" correctly, so giving every move their full energy came easily. The dance looked nearly flawless until the one-minute mark.

Suddenly, Jenn and Leila, who were supposed to do identical tumbling passes across the field on one side, collided with Carley and Marcy. Jenn accidentally added in an extra back handspring on her tumbling pass, causing her to go farther than usual, and all four girls crumpled and fell onto the soft grass like a set of dominoes. The crowds on both sides gasped, and the magic spell was broken. Coach Steele watched, holding her breath, as all the girls stood up again, unharmed.

They finished the routine as best they could, but the damage had been done. Karen Gelb and the rest of the Bulldogs were looking at them as if they weren't even cheerleaders, let alone competitors in the same division.

"Ouuuuch," Emily wailed as they jogged back to their side of the field.

Coach Steele fussed, looking over everyone like a mother hen. She was tough on them, but when it came to safety, she was always very protective. "You all right? Is anyone hurt?"

"Only our egos," said Leila, showing her human side for once. "But it's obvious that the reason we messed up is because Jenn tried to make her tumbling pass all fancy with that extra back handspring, like Devin was telling her to do."

"Let's not point any fingers," Coach said, inspecting Marcy's ankle.

Chloe narrowed her eyes and hoped Devin had learned her lesson about messing with teaching people tricks they weren't ready for. Their horrible mistake stung even worse after watching Breckenridge take to the field.

Only a few seconds into the routine, the Dogs tossed two of their girls up into the air, where they executed a pair of flawless toe touch basket tosses, as two others down front began a perfectly in-sync tumbling combo. The stands erupted in applause and shouts of encouragement. The Northside stands grew quiet.

Gemma's jaw dropped. "Oh. My. Gawd."

"They're so good, it's scary." Kalyn's eyes grew wide.

"I want to look like that!" Carley cried out. "Why don't we look like that?"

"You guys, we seriously need to step it up," Devin said, unable to tear her eyes away from the routine.

"Seriously," Chloe echoed.

At long last, it seemed the two cocaptains had finally come to an agreement on something.

CHAPTER 12

The computers in the school library were all occupied. Of course, no one was using them to do homework. There were only six old hand-me-down Macs available for student use. They crashed often and weren't good for anything other than light research or instant messaging. Kate watched for someone to finish up, so she could pounce and take the next open spot. No one was budging.

Kate scribbled her name on the sign-up sheet and sat down.

Her Beginning French textbook, *Bienvenue!*, lay on the table, unopened. It was weird that she was having trouble doing homework these days, since she usually enjoyed schoolwork, but lately her mind was on another planet. Planet Adam. She idly doodled pictures of daisies and stars on her spiral notepad and ended up writing out the name *ADAM FINDLAY*. It looked alien in her handwriting, all loopy and bubbly. She stared at it for a second, then crossed it out. Kate looked over both shoulders to check if anyone had seen. They hadn't.

Sitting next to him in Advanced English was interesting. Their start had been rocky, but somewhere along the way, his teasing had become slightly endearing. Kate suspected that Adam's constant comments on the fact that she was a cheerleader were less judgments and more excuses to talk to her. She may not have been sure if she liked him or not, but she did know that every time she headed to English she began to feel very anxious and nervous. It felt suspiciously crush-like.

She looked forward to the way he called her a secret geek and asked for her opinion on the previous night's reading each morning. But surely he wasn't really interested in her. . . . He was a junior. A cool junior. A cool junior who could do a standing back tuck better than she could. And even if he did like her—then what? She really needed to talk to Chloe. She would know what to do. Good thing Chloe had a brand-new smartphone that she could instant message on from anywhere, as long as she was in a place where a teacher wouldn't notice.

A girl with short chestnut hair tapped her on the shoulder. She was in Kate's biology class. "Your turn."

"Oh, thanks!" Kate gathered her things quickly and walked to the station in front of the window. Outside, she could see a group of rowdy seniors, including Emily's brother Chris, walking through the quad to leave campus. It was a long-standing tradition at Northside that the seniors got out of school twenty minutes before everyone else. Mainly so that they didn't have to deal with the traffic in the parking lot, but it also made them feel special. There were a lot of perks for upperclassmen. In addition to the obvious ones like prom and Ditch Day, they also got open lunch, so they could leave campus to get food. Adam never left campus for lunch, though. Kate always saw him across the quad, hanging at a picnic table with a group of his friends. A few of the times she'd looked at him, he'd been looking back.

Kate had been logged on to her messenger for less than twenty seconds before Chloe pinged her first.

> TimberChloeD: hey k8!
> LadyKate25: Yo Chlo! I was just going to message you!!
> TimberChloeD: o ya?
> LadyKate25: Need your advice on a boy situation.

LadyKate25: So confused.

TimberChloeD: k8 has a boy?! U have been holdin out on me!

LadyKate25: Well you have been pretty preoccupied lately!

TimberChloeD: tell me about it cheerleading has taken over my life even more than before
with all of the Devin drama especially…

LadyKate25: Oh yeah…: /

TimberChloeD: ugh, she's so annoying anyway, still freaking out about that bulldogs routine

LadyKate25: They were sooo amazing!

TimberChloeD: I kno, that's what scares me

LadyKate25: Don't worry, we will be too.
We have plenty of time b4 regionals.

TimberChloeD: no! something's got 2 be done now

TimberChloeD: emergency damage-control fro-yo meeting at swirls?

LadyKate25: Em too?

TimberChloeD: course! c u there at 4!

Kate signed off, feeling a little defeated. She'd wanted to ask her best friend's advice about her crush on a mysterious, geeky upperclassman. But, as usual, conversation had turned to the squad instead. Kate understood that Chloe was under a lot of pressure, taking her role as cocaptain very seriously. Maybe frozen yogurt was just the thing to cool everyone down and have a little noncheer fun. She could get Chloe's and Emily's takes on the Adam situation then.

❀

After leaving the library computer lab, Kate decided it was time to finally ditch some of her books in her locker. She hated not having everything with her at all times, but Adam did have a point about her monster bag. It was starting to make her back ache. Or maybe it was from learning new stunts. Either way, she needed to lighten up.

Devin bounded up to her from her own locker just a few rows down the hall. "Hey, Kate! Want to walk out together?" she asked.

"Yeah, of course," Kate replied with a smile. She saw no reason to be rude to Devin, who was just trying to make friends. Plus, Kate had loads of time until she had to meet Chloe and Emily at Swirls. "Does your mom pick you up from school?"

"Nah, she has to work late at the hospital. On Wednesdays, I've been walking down to the park. Usually, I just grab a soda and sit on a bench to do my homework before I walk the rest of the way home." Devin slumped against the lockers. "I don't like being home alone too much."

"Why not?" Kate asked, genuinely interested. She realized she hadn't spent much time getting to know Devin outside of cheerleading. Maybe because Chloe was always giving Kate sideways glances if she spent too long chatting with the new girl.

"It just doesn't feel like my house, you know?" Devin let out a large sigh.

"I totally understand. I have three younger half siblings. Every time I go home, it's like entering the ball pit at Kid-Zone." Kate slammed the locker shut, and they started to walk down the corridor. "Just constant noise and things getting thrown at your face."

Devin laughed. "Like what sort of things?" she asked, trying to imagine that many kids in one house. Maybe she didn't have it so bad with just her mom and Emerald, after all.

"Well, yesterday it was a powdered doughnut as soon as I walked in the door. I had confectioners' sugar in my eye for, like, twenty minutes."

"Oh, that's rough!" Devin laughed as they walked out into the sunshine. Kate noticed how pretty Devin's fiery red hair was, sparkling in the afternoon sun.

"Tell me about it!" Kate said. "Still love the kids, though."

The two girls had reached the front entrance and hesitated before parting ways. "Hey." Devin shifted back and forth on her feet. "Do you want to come to the park with me? We can sit far away from all the little kids, I promise. It will be so quiet. Nothing getting thrown at you at all—I swear!"

Devin looked so hopeful.

"That sounds fun, but I actually kinda have to be somewhere," Kate finally confessed. It made her feel really guilty for some reason. "Maybe next Wednesday, on our day off from practice?"

"Oh yeah. Totally! No big deal." Devin was noticeably disappointed. She hoisted her backpack up onto her shoulder and gave a weak smile. "See ya tomorrow." She was halfway across the parking lot when Kate had a sudden change of heart. What would it hurt to invite her to Swirls? They were basically friends now. And Chloe's issues with Devin seemed petty. She would just have to deal with it somehow.

"Hey, Devin!" yelled Kate.

Devin spun around on her heel. "Yeah?"

"Do you like frozen yogurt?"

CHAPTER 13

The best part about Swirls, the trendy new frozen yogurt place in Sunny Valley, was the fact that it was self-service. It meant that you could load up your bowl and try out all sorts of different combos without anyone giving you a sideways glance, and they had twenty flavors, like Birthday Cake Batter, Peanut Butter Explosion, strawberry, and EuroTart, and tons of toppings.

Before Chloe had even walked through the doors of the neon-green-and-white shop, she'd decided that she was going to have a EuroTart-and-strawberry combo topped with kiwis, blueberries, rainbow sprinkles, and mini gummy bears. All her favorite treats with her two favorite girls. Just what she needed to relax on their day off from cheerleading practice.

"Thanks for the ride, Mom," Chloe said as she unbuckled her seat belt to climb out of Joanie Davis's Mercedes. "I'll be home in a few hours."

"You already finished your Spanish homework?" her mom asked again, flipping her short blond hair and checking out her reflection in the rearview mirror. With her cute turned-up nose and dainty features, she was clearly Chloe's mother. She still had on her dark purple button-down and crisp gray work pants from a day at the office. "I don't want you getting kicked off the squad for poor grades. It would be *such* a shame."

Chloe sighed heavily and slumped down in her seat. They had been talking about grades since the second Chloe had arrived home from school. Just because a girl got one little C in seventh grade did not make her a total slacker. "It's still only the beginning of the year, Mom. I did great on the first two pop quizzes," Chloe replied. She was itching to get out of the car and go meet her friends. "And yes—I did the homework already. Are you happy?"

"I just want the best for you, that's all," her mother said, looking her straight in the eye. It was one of her power moves. "By the way, Jake and Clem are coming to the homecoming game just to see you, now that you're captain."

"Cocaptain," Chloe reminded her.

"Well, maybe next year you'll do better," her mom said.

Chloe shrugged. She felt like a little rain cloud had settled over her again. Her mom really had a way with words. Obviously, Joanie Davis could use a few lessons in cheerleading, specifically on how to offer encouragement.

"It wasn't really my fault, though, Mom," Chloe said, attempting to open up about Devin stealing her spotlight. They had hardly talked at all lately, so Chloe wasn't surprised that her mom didn't understand the situation. "See, there's that new girl, Devin Isle. She knew Coach Steele because her mom—"

Chloe was promptly cut off by a cell phone ring. "Yes?" Joanie answered the device, holding her hand up to Chloe in the universal sign for "hold on." "Well, get the files back to us immediately, then! I don't care that Paul went home sick and took them with him! You make him come back right now," Joanie bellowed into the phone. "Look, maybe I can swing by. Okay. Yes. Bye."

Joanie flipped her hair again and turned the key in the ignition. She was oblivious to her daughter's disappointment.

"I have to get back to the office," Joanie said, unlocking the car doors and motioning for Chloe to exit the vehicle. "So scoot! Have fun with Emily and Kate. Tell them to say hi to their mothers for me." Joanie handed Chloe a crisp twenty-dollar bill from her leather folio wallet. Chloe took the money and got out, annoyed at the predictability of her mother's attitude.

Once Chloe opened the door to Swirls, the cool rush of AC on full blast almost knocked her over. She never understood why they didn't keep it a little warmer in there so people would want to buy more frozen yogurt. It was only logical.

Chloe could hear laughter coming from the back of the store. It was definitely Emily. She was impressed that her friends were early for once.

"H-e-l-l-o!" Chloe exclaimed as she came around the corner and nearly fell over a nearby table. Emily and Kate were sitting in a booth, directly across from Devin. The three of them had already gotten their fro-yos and were sitting around chatting as if Chloe didn't exist. Chloe thought she heard Devin say the words *homecoming date*.

"Hey, Chloe! We saved you a seat!" Devin said, her mouth full of Chocolate Avalanche and crushed peanut butter cups. She patted the green plastic seat beside her. "Come on!"

What, they were suddenly best friends now? Chloe looked back and forth from Emily to Kate for an explanation, but neither of them showed any sign that they thought it was odd for Devin to be sitting with them. Maybe they had run into her there and were just playing it cool.

"I'm just going to go get some yogurt first," Chloe responded curtly. "Since you guys didn't wait."

"Don't be long!" Emily chirped. "We have a ton to go over."

As she dished up her dessert, Chloe started to seethe. She didn't want Devin there. All she had wanted was one afternoon to regroup and figure things out. She wanted to try to come up with a plan to bring up at practice, not to have Devin right there to listen and have input, too. Why was Devin Isle trying to hijack her life? First, it was captain, and now she was clearly trying to steal Chloe's best friends. This officially sucked.

Chloe was so distracted she filled up her cup with twice as much fro-yo and toppings as usual. When she weighed it at the counter, the total came to $8.72. She handed over the twenty that her mom had given her and vowed to save the rest for her charitable donation to the "Save NHS Cheerleading" fund.

"Dang, girl. Look at that thing!" Emily dug her spoon into Chloe's cup, stealing a massive clump of strawberries and gummy bears. After she had savored the bite, she turned to Chloe and said, "Verdict is: delicious. In case you wondered."

"Thanks, Em." Chloe forced a smile and dug into her creation. Maybe a little sugar would make her less grumpy. "So what's up?" She turned to Devin, trying to be casual.

"Did I hear you mention something about a date?" In truth, Chloe couldn't care less about who Devin liked. But at least she was steering the conversation away from the team.

"We were just talking about homecoming," Kate offered as she let down her dark hair from its tight bun. It fell around her shoulders and onto her green V-neck tee. A tiny gold necklace with a pendant of the bear from the California state flag hung delicately between her collarbones. "Devin was just saying that she doesn't want to go."

"Yeah, and I was just saying how I haven't had any time to look for a hot date because I've been so busy planning the dang thing," Emily said. "What's a girl to do?"

"You were so crazy to volunteer for that job in the first place," Chloe said. "I feel like I have a full plate, and I'm only doing cheerleading and schoolwork."

"It's not so bad. The lunch meetings are kinda fun. I get to choose a lot of the decorations." Emily stole more of her friend's yogurt. Chloe didn't protest.

"Oh, and we finally voted on the band—Hashtag is definitely going to perform!" She squealed in delight.

"Yay!" Kate cheered. "That's going to be so cool!"

"Who's Hashtag?" Devin asked meekly, taking another bite of yogurt. She had clammed up a bit since Chloe arrived.

"It's this group of junior guys," Kate told her. "They are going to be *big* stars."

"So is Emily once she joins forces with them," Chloe added. Emily beamed.

Devin was impressed. "So you're going to sing with them?"

"You knows it, Dev," Emily said, flipping her hair like a rock star. "Though when I go solo, I'm hoping to be a little less Gwen Stefani... and more Adele. Hashtag's sound is a little punky for my taste."

"Whatever *that* means," Kate teased.

"But back to the date thing, I'm thinking maybe Dean Stratford will ask me to the dance," Emily said, touching her hair. "Did you see the way he was flirting with me at the Medham game?"

"Yeah, I think everyone in the stands saw," Chloe said. She and Kate loved to tease Em about her boy-craziness. It was unusual that Emily hadn't secured a date yet, since flirting with boys was one of her top priorities.

"What about you guys?" Emily asked. Suddenly everyone was avoiding eye contact.

"No and thank you to that," Chloe chimed in. "I am so done with boys. All they do is disappoint you." She made a fake-wistful expression and held her hands to her chest like an old-timey Southern belle. "Besides, cheerleading is my life now."

"Devin? You seen anyone you like at school?" Kate asked, trying to include her. Devin fidgeted with her spoon and empty cup.

"No, no. Like I said, I'm not going to the dance anyway." The way Devin looked down at the table as she said it was a dead giveaway that there was more to the story.

"But you have to!" Chloe turned to Devin.

"You want me to go to the dance?" Devin replied, confused. Wasn't Chloe's main objective in life to get rid of her?

"Well, no, not exactly," Chloe said, trying not to sound like a jerk but still managing to. "I just mean that it's mandatory for squad members to attend all school events. How can we expect the other students to go if we don't set a good example?" Chloe was right—one of the biggest rules of the contract was to show support for your school by attending all the major events. Which included the much-buzzed-about homecoming dance.

"Oh, right." Devin slumped. She hadn't considered that she'd be forced to go to the dance. In fact, she'd been hoping to avoid the night altogether. She hadn't even mentioned it to Josh, but he probably couldn't come anyway. "I'm not bringing a date, though. There's no way my boyfriend could come all the way down here from the Bay."

"You have a boyfriend and you didn't tell us?!" Emily leaned over. "What's his name? Is he cute? Tell us everything."

Devin didn't really feel like doing this, but there was no way out of it. "His name's Josh."

"Josh what?" Emily said, clicking on her cell.

"Josh Griffith. Why?"

"I'm Facebooking him. I want to see what he looks like," Emily replied like it was no big deal. She tapped away at her screen.

"No!" Devin shouted, then lowered her voice. "I mean, I'll show you a good one later."

Emily scoffed. "Whoa, what's the big deal?"

"Oh, leave her alone, Em," Kate said. She understood Devin's hesitation at spilling all of her boy details. That stuff could be so embarrassing. And Devin obviously had a reason she was keeping it safe.

"Thanks." Devin smiled at Kate. It felt weird discussing Josh with these girls when he knew nothing about their existence. It was almost as if Devin had been trying to keep her entire life a secret until she was ready to reveal her new cheerleader identity to him. She didn't want to be tagged in some sort of cheerleading picture online and have him find out like that, either. Devin made a mental note to disable tagging on her profile when she got home.

"Well, anyway, it looks like we're all dateless," Chloe said, satisfied. "That's actually great! We can just have fun together."

Devin smiled. She assumed this meant she was included.

Kate held back from mentioning Adam. It wasn't as if he'd asked her to the dance or anything... but she wondered what it would be like if he did.

"Now we have more time to focus on our routine,"

Chloe proclaimed. She hit the table with her fist like it was a gavel and she was holding court. The empty yogurt cups rattled.

"So what are we gonna do?" Emily said. "I heard some of the Breckenridge girls saying they were coming to our homecoming game just to see us crash again."

"Seriously?" Devin asked. "That's messed up."

"Don't worry—I told them that they *should* come and watch us blow their minds," Emily added casually.

Chloe's face turned white. "What!" They hadn't even started on a new routine yet, and now Emily was going around making bold claims about how great it was going to be. Chloe had to hand it to her—Emily had said she wanted more guts and she'd followed through. "Em—what have you done now?" Chloe put her face in her hands.

"We'll just have to come up with something. We always do," Kate said as she began to gather the empty cups.

It pained her to admit it, but Chloe confessed, "I literally have no idea what to do."

Kate and Emily turned to Devin. "Cocaptain? Any thoughts?"

"Well, I was watching some of Sage's old routines on DVD at home, and I did see a few things that we could try..." Devin started, testing the waters. All three girls hung on her every word.

"Have you guys ever heard of a tic-tock?" Devin asked.

"I think our squad could definitely pull it off with a little practice. I'm sure I could ask my sister for some tips...."

"Keep talking," Chloe said, rapt with attention.

Twenty minutes later, the four of them had hunkered down and made a plan together. Chloe had to admit that Devin had proved herself to be a bit useful. If only Chloe had appreciated her sooner.

CHAPTER 14

Over the next week, practices started to resemble the more intense training sessions of a college team rather than a casual after-school extracurricular. Everyone was feeling the effects. "If we try this stunt again, I swear my arms are going to turn into actual jelly," Kalyn whined, rubbing her forearms. Half of her shiny black hair had come loose from its ponytail, and her legs were dotted with tiny bruises. The rest of the squad seemed to be in similar shape. Everyone was exhausted from attempting the tic-tock. The advanced stunt required the top girls to switch their supporting leg while being held up in the air by their bases.

"Have you seen these bruises on my leg from where

Emily landed on me yesterday?" Arianna exclaimed, pointing to a set of massive multicolored patches.

"Whoa, double rainbow...all the way across your thigh!" Emily joked, referencing a YouTube video she'd seen a billion times. "But seriously—I *am* sorry about that."

"Just one more time, guys!" Chloe clapped her hands in encouragement. "Come on, we're so close to nailing it."

"Chloe's right—we can't quit now," Devin reaffirmed, doing her best to support her cocaptain. Devin was figuring out how to work with Chloe. It was all about choosing her moments and choosing her battles. It was easier said than done, but the approach seemed to be working so far. And if she was going to keep up with cheerleading, why not try to make their relationship better?

"Devin?" Chloe said. "Would you spot this one? I want to see what it looks like from the other angle, too. Football fields do have a three-hundred-and-sixty-degree view, you know."

"You bet," said Devin, jogging to the back of the mats.

"Can we please get it right this time, girls?" Carley whined. She pointed to the captains. "These two are crazy."

"Oh, be quiet," Jenn replied. "We all want to win, right?"

"Well, duh. What a genius concept, Jenn," Leila remarked. *"Winning."* She had been suspiciously quiet throughout practice. She only seemed to thrive when there was conflict present, so naturally she must have been feeling a little bummed when she saw Devin and Chloe getting along so well for the first time. Her little plan to knock Chloe from power by pitting Devin against her was starting to backfire.

"Great work, guys!" Chloe shouted when the grueling session finally came to a close. They still had a way to go but had definitely shown some improvement. That was all that mattered today. Coach Steele watched from the front of the mats. The look on her face was a mixture of pride and *I told you so* directed at the two captains, which Chloe did her best to ignore. Just because they were getting along right now did not mean that Chloe agreed with Coach's choice to let Devin share her role.

Coach made a motion for everyone to sit down on the mats. "Everyone listen up—Emily Arellano has an extremely important announcement to make. If you don't listen— that's a demerit." As usual, Kate stiffened at the mention of demerits, even though Coach Steele was joking. "Emily, the floor is yours."

"I know you're all super-tired and want to collapse, so I'll make this quick." In truth, Emily was the one who looked like she was about to collapse. She mustered enough energy to hold up a clipboard. "The Northside JV cheer squad is having a bake sale! Everyone is expected to bake something delicious and bring it to the sale, since half of the proceeds will go to our charity of the season, Hearts Heal, and the other half to our competition fees for Regionals."

"And Nationals!" Coach Steele added, holding up her hand to show her crossed fingers.

"I love bake sales!" Gemma said. "I'm going to make red velvet cupcakes."

"Can I make rainbow-sprinkle cupcakes?" Lexi asked, raising her hand.

"Sounds great! I don't care what you guys make, just please remember to do it. This is for your community and your team," Emily reminded everyone.

"I'm going to just buy something," Leila said. "I hate baking. All that fat and sugar near you. Ugh." Leila shuddered.

"Mandatory, everyone," Coach Steele reiterated. "That means you *have* to do it. And no store-bought items!"

"Well, I love baking," Marcy replied. "I'll make your cake for you, Leila."

"Fine," said Leila. "But make something good."

Devin waited patiently till the sign-up sheet reached her. Almost everyone on the list seemed to be making cupcakes. How boring. *Strawberry-rhubarb pie*, Devin wrote, thinking maybe she'd better make one tonight as practice. It was Josh's favorite dessert, so she'd made it once before for his birthday, since he said he wasn't a "cake guy." In addition to not being a "team-sports guy," he also wasn't a "cheese guy" or a "swimming guy." But, Devin thought, he was a "Devin guy," and that was what really mattered. Maybe it was finally time to tell him about cheerleading and the pact that she'd made with her mom. He couldn't be mad when she broke the news that they'd be able to spend New Year's Eve together so long as she stayed on the squad.

❋

Twenty minutes later, Devin was walking home when a silver Prius pulled up next to her. The passenger window rolled down slowly. "Get in, and we'll give you a ride," Leila said, sounding almost friendly.

Devin was hot and tired from practice, and the promise of air-conditioning seemed like heaven. "No, I'm all right just walking," said Devin, looking at Leila suspiciously. She still wasn't sure whether she could trust the girl. It seemed like one minute Leila was trying to be someone's friend, and the next she was making mean comments behind that person's back. Devin still didn't understand what Leila had gained by trying to get her elected as captain.

"Oh, cut the crap, Devin," Leila said. "You totally want a ride, so stop pretending that you don't." Leila reached back and opened the back car door. "Get in!"

"Fine," Devin said as she climbed into the backseat and

buckled up. "Thanks. Hi, I'm Devin." She reached across to shake Mrs. Savett's hand.

Mrs. Savett smiled back. She shared Leila's dark hair and blue eyes, but her expression was warmer than her daughter's. "It's so nice to meet you! I have heard so much about the talented new girl from the Bay! Leila told me about your wonderful tumbling skills."

"She did?" Devin was puzzled. Leila didn't seem to like Devin that much, and now she was raving about her impressive cheerleading talents to her mother? Leila turned around in her seat and smiled sweetly, batting her eyelashes. Okay, so it was all just an elaborate act for her mom's sake. That made more sense.

"Yeah, Mom. Remember when I told you about that girl that Chloe was trying to get kicked off the squad? This is her!"

Devin's heart dropped into her stomach. "What are you talking about?"

Leila turned around again, her blue eyes sparkling innocently. "Oh, no. This is so awkward." Leila let her long, brown locks down from her practice ponytail and tried to smooth out the big crease. "I thought you knew about that."

"No," Devin said, feeling the blood drain from her face. "No, I didn't know that at all. Tell me everything."

Twenty minutes later, Devin was sitting in Leila Savett's

palatial bedroom thinking, *How did I get here?* It was decorated entirely in green with silver accents. A queen-sized bed with a canopy stood at its center, dressed with a forest-hued brocade duvet. A tiara-shaped throw pillow was tossed carelessly on the floor, and discarded clothes covered every surface of the room. A black modern shelf displayed several trophies with tiny gold cheerleaders in different positions on top of them. Prize ribbons of red and blue lined the side of a silver-framed full-length mirror on the wall, alongside snapshots of Leila in an all-star uniform.

Leila sat down at her desk—which was covered in lipgloss tubes and small jars of expensive-looking cosmetics, rather than homework—and logged on to her laptop. Devin immediately regretted being talked into coming upstairs.

"I tried to warn you about Chloe Davis, but you wouldn't listen," Leila said matter-of-factly. "She will stop at nothing to have all the glory to herself."

"She is pretty determined, but I don't know that I would go that far. Are you sure she was actually trying to get me kicked off the team?" Devin asked.

"Why would I lie about that?"

"You tell me," Devin replied, shrugging. "It seems like you and Chloe go way back." Devin stood up to inspect a picture of the Sunny Valley All-Stars. Chloe and Leila were right at the center, done up in bright makeup and smiling, arms around each other. Devin pointed to the picture. "What about this picture? Looks like you guys are close."

"That was in the past," Leila replied. There was no trace of nostalgia in her voice. "You know, before she got all full of herself." Leila turned back to her computer and tapped away at it. "Anyway, come here and look. Proof."

Devin leaned over Leila's shoulder to view the screen. It was open to an e-mail. Devin scanned the page, her curiosity growing.

September 15 5:07 PM
TO: <"JV Team">
FROM: <"Chloe Davis">
SUBJECT: Are we going to allow this?

Hey ladies,
We need to do something! This is so not fair that Devin was allowed to join the team. She is not even any good. Coach Steele only wants her around because she feels bad for her. This is bad for us. We really have to win Regionals this year, and if we have to teach her everything, it will take precious time away from our practice. Let's stand up and tell Coach we want her gone!
—Chloe

P.S. Her practice clothes are hideous, too.

Devin's heart sank. She knew that Chloe was having a hard time sharing the spotlight, but she hadn't realized it was this bad. And despite their differences, Chloe seemed like a friendly, good-hearted girl. Not the type who would send a mass e-mail that was so plain...nasty. The words really stung.

Leila quickly closed the laptop and turned to Devin. "The truth hurts, huh?"

"Nope," Devin lied. "I don't care."

She wasn't going to let Chloe's e-mail scare her off. From now on, she was going to run things like she wanted to—no more tiptoeing around Chloe's feelings. Devin had been elected fair and square by her teammates, and she owed it to them to do her best.

"Hey, Leila?" Devin asked. "Would you mind forwarding that e-mail to me?"

"I'd rather not," Leila answered. "I don't want to get in the middle of it, you know?" When Devin finally arrived home that night, she couldn't help thinking that Leila was "in the middle of it" whether she liked it or not.

CHAPTER 15

Four minutes had passed since Kate had done anything but chew on her left index fingernail. With only twenty-two minutes left in the period, she'd written half of what she needed for her timed essay about Hester Prynne. For some reason, Kate was really having trouble characterizing the relationship between Hester and the Reverend Arthur Dimmesdale, even though she'd read *The Scarlet Letter* twice before—once on her own and another time during a summer course at the community college. *Focus!* she urged herself, and visualized a completed essay on the desk in front of her. Chloe had been trying to teach her the technique. Maybe it only worked for cheerleading moves.

Adam's presence next to her wasn't helping—today he'd worn a blue-and-gold-plaid shirt and looked extremely adorable. She wondered if the color choice was just a coincidence or if she'd actually inspired him to have some school spirit. It was a game-day Friday, after all. Kate secretly hoped it was the latter. She got a special satisfaction from seeing typically unspirited kids joining in on spirit days. It also made Kate's stomach twist to think that maybe he'd worn it because of her. She stole a glance at him and decided that the shirt was intentional.

"Fifteen more minutes," Mrs. Lawrence announced to the class without looking up from the stack of papers she was grading. Kate snapped out of her daydream and looked at her half-blank page. If she was going to finish on time, she needed to be working, not staring at a boy. That wasn't who she was at all.

Kate had just scribbled a quote from *The Scarlet Letter*—"*She had not known the weight until she felt the freedom*"—when she felt something hit her cheer shoe. It was a small piece of paper rolled up like a scroll. A wrinkled blue twist tie edged in silver held it together.

"Hey!" Adam whispered across the aisle, pointing to the scroll. She wasn't sure if the note was meant for her or if he'd just dropped it and it had accidentally rolled her way. Passing notes in class was so old-fashioned. Normally, kids sneaked texts to each other when the teacher's back was turned. But whatever this was, it looked important. Like an invitation to a party or something. Kate fumbled to pick it up, pretending to drop her pencil in the process. It was probably overkill, but she faked a cough to mask the move as well.

She made sure Mrs. Lawrence wasn't looking and leaned across the aisle. "Pssst—here!" she whispered back, but Adam was now hunched over his own essay, writing away like nothing had happened. "Adam?" she whispered again, but he kept looking down at his desk. The scroll felt like it was burning a hole in her palm. Mrs. Lawrence shot her a be-quiet-or-else look. Kate discreetly slipped the scroll into her backpack. She would just have to give it to him later.

It was lucky that Mrs. Lawrence said Kate could have an extra ten minutes to finish her essay, because she had wasted the last fifteen minutes of the period thinking about Adam and the mysterious note. Adam obviously hadn't had the same problem concentrating, since he turned his essay in right when the bell rang, and then left.

The hallway was mostly empty by the time Kate got to her locker. This time was technically reserved for homeroom, but once the students checked in, the teachers would usually let them spend the twenty-minute period out on the grassy areas of the quad, enjoying cups of coffee and snacks from the cafeteria cart and joking around. Kate's friends were probably already sitting out in their favorite spot under a big, shady tree, but she decided to walk to her locker for a moment of privacy.

Kate reached into her bag and removed her English binder, which was covered in a collage of cheerleading photos she'd taken from Chloe's website. Her fingers grazed the little paper scroll. Kate wanted a better look at the note, maybe even to read it. Maybe if she tied it back exactly how it was before, Adam would never know.

A couple of students walked past Kate, laughing. She huddled over the little piece of paper, even though they had no idea what she was doing. She read the messy handwriting.

"Screw your courage to the sticking-place!"
words that ring true
Be a Man and ask her
while donning gold and blue

It didn't make much sense. Kate recognized the line about courage from *Macbeth*, but the rest was hardly Shakespeare. Was this some sort of riddle? Was it possible that this was actually meant for her? Adam *had* been wearing gold and blue, but that didn't mean much. Then Kate noticed a tiny line at the bottom of the page. It said:

Lady Kate—will you go to homecoming with me?
—Lord Adam
P.S. I hope this isn't too cheesy.

Her heart quickened. Kate caught her reflection in her tiny locker mirror and could see that her face was beginning to flush red. She felt excited and scared at the same time.

They would probably go to a nice dinner with his friends before the dance. She'd be wearing a pretty dress but would probably spill something on it. Or say the wrong thing or get food stuck in her teeth. Or accidentally wear heels that made her taller than him. Or do any number of embarrassing things, really. Adam would regret bringing the awkward freshman, and they'd never talk again.

The fact that he'd asked her made Kate feel special, but Adam was cool in a way that she'd never be. He was smart, collected, and funny. If she said yes, she worried she'd end up being a disappointment.

Kate slammed her locker shut and hurried outside to meet her friends. At least there were a few minutes left to relax before the next class. Chloe was sitting on a blanket on the grass, and Emily was pacing around, telling her a story with elaborate hand gestures.

"Kate!" Emily exclaimed. She took a sip of her coffee and nibbled on a granola bar. "How was your crazy English class for geniuses?"

"It was pretty good." Kate took a seat on the grass. "And actually *quite* eventful."

"Did you fail a test or something?" Chloe joked, gesturing with her cup of Greek yogurt. "Because *that* would be eventful."

"Well, maybe now that you mention it..." Kate unpeeled a banana and took a large bite. "But that's not what I meant."

Chloe looked at Kate quizzically. She didn't love the guessing game. Chloe always got straight to the point. "So, what then?"

"Someone sort of...asked me to homecoming?" Kate admitted shyly. She considered showing them the scroll note but decided against it. That felt like something she should keep to herself. At least for now, while she figured out her feelings a little better.

"Whoa. Go, Kate!" Emily shouted. She stood up and made a victory sign with her arms as if she were cheering on Kate instead of the football players. "Who is it? Is he on the team?"

Kate shook her head. "Nope...not on the team."

"Is it that sophomore Brad Bell? At the game against Medham, I saw him sitting in the stands, staring at your chest during every. Single. Cheer," Emily said matter-of-factly. Emily always seemed to know who liked whom at any given moment. It was a silly skill, in Kate's opinion. Especially since the stats changed on a daily basis.

"That is so not true, Em." Kate looked down at her less-than-impressive chest. "I mean, come on. Really? Do you even hear what you are saying?"

"Well, tell us, then!" Chloe urged. "Who is the new secret boyfriend? Oh! Is it that guy you mentioned online last week?"

"He's not my boyfriend at all! And it doesn't matter anyway, because I'm not going to the dance with him," Kate announced. She looked off across the large concrete quad, hoping to catch a glimpse of Adam's blue-and-gold shirt somewhere in the area where the juniors hung out. It was a blur of blue and gold everywhere, though, so for once he blended in. "We all said we'd go together without dates, right?"

Chloe shrugged and Emily rolled her eyes. "Stop being so uptight! Isn't there some poem about how you turn boring when all you do is work?"

Kate took another bite of banana. "'All work and no play makes Jack a dull boy'?"

"Yes! That's you. You're Jack," Emily sassed back. "Learn to loosen up! What grade is he in?" Emily smoothed down her cheerleading skirt and knelt next to Kate like a little kid waiting for story time.

"Well, he's a junior...." Kate supposed she couldn't blame Emily for digging for information, since Kate was the one who'd brought it up. Luckily, the warning bell rang before Kate had to answer any more questions. Kate thought of introducing Adam to her friends and imagined how they'd react. Chloe and Emily probably wouldn't want her dating an English geek like him, even if he was a junior. They tended to gravitate more toward sporty guys, like Dean Stratford from the JV football team. Adam was totally different from Dean in every way. *And that's part of his charm*, Kate thought.

"You better tell us more tonight at the game!" Chloe yelled as she tossed her yogurt cup into a blue NHS trash can. "Or you get a demerit!"

"Very funny!" Kate shouted back at her. "You wish you had that power!"

CHAPTER 16

Later that night, the dusky Southern California sky settled in over the Northside football stadium. The air was warm and there was a buzz of excitement in the stands. It was an absolutely perfect night for football. Neither the El Dorado High Mavericks nor the Northside Timberwolves had scored so far, but the JV cheerleaders were keeping the fans excited. With the homecoming game against Elliot High fast approaching, the pressure was on the football team to win at least one game. Chloe was beginning to take it personally that the squad's cheers hadn't had any effect on the boys whatsoever.

When a time-out was called in the second quarter,

Devin yelled to the team. "We need to project louder, girls!" Kalyn nodded in agreement as Devin continued. "We want the guys out there to hear us, too. Not just the people in the stands." She clapped her hands together loudly. "Come on, Wolves!"

Chloe chimed in. "The point is for us to lead the fans in cheers so that then the team can hear all of us." She knew what she was saying sounded really obvious, but she couldn't stop herself from disagreeing with Devin.

"But *everyone* should hear us, right?" Devin replied. Several of the girls stopped listening.

"Ugh, I can't take this bickering anymore," said Carley, shaking her head in defeat.

Lately, it seemed like every time Devin gave a tip or a pointer to the team, Chloe had some sort of opposing comment. And vice versa. Most of the time, they weren't even constructive. The halftime routine for homecoming was the perfect example: they'd already switched the stunt sequences four times because Chloe and Devin couldn't agree on what looked better.

Coach Steele had taken a hands-off approach to the disagreements, saying that the spirit of teamwork was learning to compromise and come together. She would let them argue their points until they reached a conclusion. But Kate could tell that even Coach's patience with Chloe and Devin's bickering was starting to wear thin, and she was too proud to admit her mistake in casting two girls in one lead role.

"Well, personally, I agree with Chloe on this one," Leila butted in. Chloe's face registered shock. Wasn't this the girl who had just come up to her at practice a few days ago and said that her choreography was "stale"? The last time Leila had been on Chloe's side, they'd been about eleven years old. Maybe Leila was feeling nostalgic.

"Shouldn't we all be focusing on cheering for our team right now instead of taking sides in petty arguments?" Devin sighed, turning to Leila.

"Weren't you two the ones who started this?" Leila said back, pointing to Chloe and Devin. "Some captains you guys are."

"Ladies!" Coach Steele shouted from the bench. "That's enough of that. Get moving!" She gestured to the stands. Several of the parents had started watching them argue. Chloe's face burned with humiliation.

"Let's do 'Truckin'!" Emily suggested to the group, naming a super-easy cheer that always got the crowd fired up. It was just what everyone needed to regain their focus. Across the field, Chloe watched the El Dorado cheerleaders perform a cheer in their red uniforms. They looked really solid. It was a wake-up call to do better.

The Northside girls picked up their poms and started to cheer.

"T! T-R-U! T-R-U-C-K! KEEP ON TRUCKIN', ALL THE WAY!" the girls yelled in unison while clapping their hands together. They repeated the cheer five times. By the end of it, the people in the stands had all started clapping, too.

"YELL N-H-S!" Chloe improvised.

"N-H-S!" the squad echoed, huge smiles on their faces. Soon enough, fans in the stands were also smiling and chanting "N-H-S!" while clapping their hands to the beat. Chloe saw it as a perfect opportunity to launch straight into another, more complex cheer.

"NORTHSIDE HIGH, LET'S BEGIN!" Chloe shouted, quickly glancing behind her to make sure the team was with her. They were mostly on point. Surprisingly, Kate was a little off. She seemed to be searching the stands for someone.

"NORTHSIDE, GO! FIGHT AND WIN!" Kalyn, Arianna, and Leila stepped forward. They pumped their right arms into the air, while their left arms remained glued to their hips.

Gemma and Carley circled their arms and brought them up to a high V, then a low V. "WE'RE TRUE! WE'RE TRUE! WE'RE BLUE! WE'RE BLUE!" they projected into the crowd.

Jenn and Devin stepped forward and repeated the same motion in reverse. "WE'RE BOLD! WE'RE BOLD! WE'RE GOLD! WE'RE GOLD!"

"BLUE AND GOLD!" everyone yelled out together as they prepped their stunt groups. "TRUE...AND BOLD!" The groups on the right and in the middle lifted their top girls into liberties, but the group on the left failed to deliver. They didn't even get Arianna off the ground. A group couldn't stunt without all its bases, and for the first time ever Kate wasn't there for her teammates.

Chloe could see Kate frozen in her formation spot up front, staring out into the crowd like a deer in headlights. Chloe had no idea what had happened. Kate never forgot cheers, and especially never during a game.

As soon as everyone's feet were back on the ground, Chloe pulled Kate aside. "What happened just then?" she asked, reaching up and putting her hand on Kate's shoulder. "Who were you looking for in the stands?"

"I wasn't—I just...I just thought I saw someone I knew, and I blanked," Kate lied. "I'm really sorry I screwed it up." Kate glanced back up toward the stands briefly. Her mind was still clearly elsewhere, and she had a dreamy look in her eyes. Chloe suddenly understood. Just one glance at Greg Marina during a cheer, and she had to work double hard to concentrate and not forget the words.

"It was that mystery junior, wasn't it?" Chloe smirked, switching from stern-captain mode to best-friend mode. "Why won't you tell us who he is?"

Kate sighed. "Because it's stupid. It's nothing."

Santa Clara County Library
District

408-293-2326

Account Status 5/14/2019 18:14

XXXXXXXXXXXXX8139

Item Title	Due Date
1. Game on : a varsity novel	6/4/2019
33305228775445	
2. Keys to the city	6/4/2019
33305239131885	
3. Tales from a not-so-secret	6/4/2019
crush catastrophe	
33305239699725	
4. Ruby in the sky	6/4/2019
33305244009986	
5. Refugee	6/4/2019
33305244792333	

No of Items: 5

Amount Outstanding: $0.50

24/7 Telecirc: 800-471-0991
www.sccl.org
Thank you for visiting our library.

Santa Clara County Library
District
408-293-2326

Account Status 6/4/2019 18:14
XXXXXXXXXX8139

Item Title	Due Date
1. Game on : a Varsity novel 33305228775445	6/4/2019
2. Keys to the city 33305239131885	6/4/2019
3. Tales from a not-so-secret crush catastrophe 33305239599725	6/4/2019
4. Ruby in the sky 33305244400986	6/4/2019
5. Refugee 33305244792333	6/4/2019

No of items: 5

Amount Outstanding: $0.00

24/7 Telecirc 800-471-0991
www.sccl.org
Thank you for visiting our library

"If Kate MacDonald is forgetting her cheers, then it clearly is something," Chloe said, trying to be gentle. "Just don't miss your stunts again, okay?"

"Totally." Kate nodded furiously. She was silently cursing herself for being so careless. "It won't happen again."

But later, during the third quarter, things weren't looking up for the girls. Coach Steele waved Devin and Chloe over during a break. "What's going on out there? Are any of your teammates paying attention?" Coach asked. Chloe took in the sight of the team. Coach Steele was right. Only half of them were even standing on the sidelines of the field, watching. The other half were either texting on the bench like Leila and Marcy, exhausted like Emily, or lovesick and spaced-out like Kate. "I'm disappointed in you two," Coach said, her voice stern. "Fix it."

For the rest of the night, Chloe felt like Coach Steele was watching her every move, waiting for her to mess up again. By the sound of the last buzzer, the scoreboard still bore a big fat 0 on the Northside section. It seemed fitting that the JV Timberwolves had lost yet another game, because Chloe was feeling like a loser, too.

CHAPTER 17

"This is torture," Josh whimpered on the chat window. "Watching my girlfriend bake my favorite dessert and I can't even be there to try it."

Devin giggled and licked the wooden spoon she was using to stir sugar into the mixture of chopped rhubarb and strawberries. Baking this pie while video chatting with Josh was definitely doing its job to cheer her up. She'd been feeling low ever since Leila had shown her Chloe's e-mail, and the squad's poor showing at last night's football game certainly hadn't helped. She knew Coach Steele had been disappointed in them. "I told you, I have to do this. It's homework!"

"For what class? How to Tease Josh 101?"

"How to Bake Awesome Pies 101." Devin laughed. She popped a piece of crust dough into her mouth.

"That's not a class. How to Be Super-Shady 101?" Josh guessed, taking a gulp of his traditional root beer.

"Home economics?" Devin raised her eyebrows. "Okay, that's a lie."

"I knew it!" Josh yelled. "The Devver would never take home ec."

"How do you know, mister?" Devin said, taking a seat on one of the tall kitchen stools.

"Because you hate traditional gender roles," Josh said simply, and he shrugged.

Devin couldn't really argue with that. "Okay, fine. That's true." She'd always been enchanted with the idea of female pilots or stay-at-home dads. There was something really inspiring about breaking out of your shell and standing against expectations like that.

Devin turned away from the camera and mysteriously looked over her shoulder. "But there's still a lot about me that you don't know. . . ."

Josh leaned forward, smiling. He clearly thought it was a game. "Oh yeah? Name one thing."

Devin's heart began to beat really fast. This was it—the conversation she'd been dreading for weeks. She could feel herself starting to chicken out. But she really needed to clue him in. How else could she tell him about her life or ask him what to do about the Chloe situation? Since Leila had revealed that Chloe had written an online rant about Devin, she'd felt like she needed guidance more than ever.

"Well...you don't know that I...hate tacos?" Devin said weakly.

"You hate tacos?" Josh said in mock shock, putting his hand to his chest like he was about to faint. "Why are we even dating?"

She laughed nervously. "Yeah. I do! I-hate-tacos-*and*-I-joined-the-Northside-JV-cheerleading-squad." It all spilled out as if it were one word.

Josh laughed hysterically. "Good one, Devver!"

"No, Josh. I'm serious."

"About the tacos?"

"No, the other thing." Devin looked down at her flour-covered hands briefly, and when she looked back up, Josh wasn't laughing anymore.

"I'm sorry, did you just tell me that you're a *cheerleader*?" Josh didn't seem to really believe the words he was saying. He frowned as if they tasted bad on his tongue. "But...I thought we hated cheerleaders. You always said—"

"I know I did," Devin said sincerely. "But I can explain! See, I'm only doing it because I made this deal with my mom that—"

"How long have you been doing this?" Josh interrupted.

He looked weird, but Devin tried to be brave. She knew this conversation was about so much more than the fact that she was a cheerleader now. It was about the elephant in the room—or two rooms, for that matter. The fact that they were living hundreds of miles apart from each other and that their lives were starting to take different directions. Neither of them wanted to admit it.

"Since school started. Like I said, it was a favor for my mom. I wasn't even going to keep doing it, but..." Devin tried to explain. "But it made her so happy! And then she told me that if I gave it a real shot, for all of football season, she would pay for you to come down and visit me during break and we could spend New Year's Eve together! So I stuck with it." He remained quiet. "I was going to tell you, I swear."

"You still lied to me, Dev," Josh said, his shoulders slumping. "I just don't know why you would do that." He took off his guitar strap and put the guitar on the floor, obviously trying to take it all in. "I wondered what you were up to after school every day."

Devin wasn't sure what to say, but she could tell he was upset. "Josh, I'm sorry, but—"

"It kind of hurts that you didn't feel like you could tell me this."

"I was nervous! After what you said about Luke joining the football team and all that stuff," Devin said, her voice small, "I thought you wouldn't respect me anymore."

"Well, I'm having a harder time doing that now."

Ouch. He did have a point, though. "I don't know what to say," Devin replied. The two of them had never had a real fight, so Devin wasn't sure how to act.

"Look, it's fine," he interrupted before she could explain any further. "We'll talk tomorrow." The chat window promptly went black. Was this really breakup-worthy? A little lie about participating in a team sport, just so she could eventually see him? This was for both of them!

Devin didn't know exactly what was going through Josh's head at the moment, but she certainly felt like she'd lost something bigger than a competition. Trust was a lot harder to earn than trophies, she knew.

CHAPTER 18

Even after a weekend away from cheer practice and dance committee planning, Emily was still tired. Third-period biology was usually her favorite class, but today she couldn't seem to keep her eyes open. Everyone was wearing pajamas to celebrate the first day of Spirit Week activities, and Emily wanted to blame her sleepiness on the fact that school looked like a bizarre slumber party. But really, she was just plain worn out.

Mr. Liu had put on a documentary about the migratory patterns of Canada geese, and Emily had laid her head down on her desk and closed her eyes. Her mind drifted to all the tasks on her homecoming to-do list. There were only a few days left! Between meeting her responsibilities on the dance committee, learning the new halftime routine for cheerleading, and managing her schoolwork, Emily felt like she was being pulled in every direction. That didn't even include the time she'd spent on her special musical side project. She had been practicing a few songs with the guys from Hashtag every weekend. Singing with them made her feel completely excited and free. It was almost as good as being thrown into a basket toss. *Almost.*

"Miss Arellano?" Mr. Liu called out to Emily, noticing she wasn't paying attention in the slightest. "During what season does the Canada goose begin its migration?"

"Um, seventeen!" she answered with a start, without even thinking. "I mean, it's a V formation! V for victory! Go, Team Goose?" Emily always hoped that making a joke could deflect a bad situation like this one. Unfortunately, Mr. Liu didn't look impressed or amused.

"Pay attention, Emily," he said, looking down through his glasses. "Just because it's a film doesn't mean it won't be on the final exam. I hope that all of your extracurricular activities aren't interfering with your schoolwork. Do I need to talk to Coach Steele?"

"Of course not," Emily said quickly.

"Good." He smiled curtly. "Now sit up straight, please."

Emily always thought that saying no to an experience

didn't get a person anywhere. If there was an extreme roller coaster in front of her, Emily would ride it. If there was an exotic food to try, she would taste it. And if someone offered her a chance to perform at homecoming in front of the entire student body, she would do it. So what if she sacrificed a few hours of sleep to fit it all in?

When the period ended, Emily rushed down the Science block and out the hallway door. She only had a few minutes to make it across campus to the final dance committee meeting. She started to jog and instantly felt silly to be running across school in her Hello Kitty pajamas.

Slowing down, she walked up the concrete steps that led into the gym and immediately spotted Travis Hollister, the lead guitarist of Hashtag, waiting by the doorway. He wasn't the type of guy Emily usually liked, but she couldn't deny that he was cute. His blond hair was cut in a way that looked sort of emo—short except for the top, with bangs that fell into his eyes when he looked down—and he managed to look clean-cut and scruffy at the same time. It was the perfect look for a guy who spent his time staring down at the strings of an electric guitar. Wearing dark skinny jeans and a plain black tee that said NHS JAZZ BAND in the corner, he clearly wasn't participating in Spirit Week. Emily thought it was awesome that he wasn't afraid to be a band geek, even though his cool Hashtag buddies often teased him for it.

"What are you doing here?" Emily called out. "Did you come to help us decide where we're putting the inflatable dragon? I named him Draco."

"Nice try, but no way. I have English with Chloe Davis, and she said you'd be here. I wanted to tell you some awesome news." He bit his lip.

"Oh yeah?" Emily brushed her fingers through her long, dark hair. She was suddenly very aware of her awkward pajama-clad appearance. "What's that?"

"So, you know how I said that my uncle does the landscaping for that talent scout Nic Aragon?"

"I thought your uncle owned the Halloween Superstore."

"No, that's Uncle Steve. This is Uncle John—he runs a landscaping company." Travis laughed. "Anyway, that doesn't matter. What I'm trying to say is—he's coming to the dance to watch us perform!"

"The talent scout or your uncle John?" Emily asked.

Travis put his face in his palm and laughed. "Come on! Isn't this amazing? We could be discovered, like, *not* on YouTube."

"Are you friggin' kidding me? That's awesome!"

Emily hadn't really thought too much about trying to get "discovered." She had fantasies of becoming a famous singer one day, of course, but she had never really considered that it could happen soon. The thought made her stomach flutter a little bit.

"Emily?" Megan O'Kelly, a fellow dance committee member, wandered out of the gym, shielding her eyes from the sun. Her face was entirely covered in freckles, and she was wearing adult-sized red footie pajamas. "I thought I heard you out here! We're all waiting inside." Travis looked at Megan, totally bewildered by her outfit.

"Sorry, gotta go!" Emily told Travis. "Dance duty calls!" She started toward the doors.

"Wait, Em?" Travis called out from halfway down the steps.

"Yeah?" She peeked her head back out the doors.

"Cute kitty pj's." He laughed and took off in the opposite direction.

"You think this is good?" she shouted after him. "Just wait till you see what I'm going to wear to the dance, Hollister!"

CHAPTER 19

"Ladies and gentlemen of Sunny Valley, welcome to the twenty-third annual Northside High School home-coming game! Please give a warm welcome to your Junior Varsity Timberwolves!" The announcer's voice blared through the stadium speakers as the blue-and-gold-clad players ran onto the field. "Give these guys a hand, folks!" The team seemed to feed off the energy of the crowd and the excitement of the occasion, running faster and standing a little taller than usual. Devin hoped that it meant they would actually score some points.

The marching band sat in full uniform in the stands, playing the school fight song over the cheers and whistles of the packed crowd. The stands were decorated with strings of blue and yellow Christmas lights and twisted crepe paper streamers. Big bunches of shimmery balloons in the school colors hung at the end of each bench, and massive white letter balloons, just like the ones at Breckenridge's homecoming, lined the top of the back row. Emily and the homecoming committee had come through.

The Northside High cheerleaders lined the sidelines. The JV team warmed up while the Varsity girls passed out paw-print face tattoos and blue "thunder sticks"—pairs of inflatable rods that made a loud noise when hit together—to the fans in the stands. Devin was amazed at the transformation of the stadium. She'd been to only two other homecoming games—one when Sage was a senior back in the Bay Area, and, more recently, the game against Breckenridge High. Being on the sidelines made the experience totally different and way more exciting than being in the stands.

"But why do the letter balloons spell *inside*?" Jenn asked as she stopped stretching and stood up for a better look. She squinted her eyes, which were expertly lined in gold eye pencil that she used only for special occasions.

Emily sighed but took the criticism in stride. "Look, I tried! We could only afford five letters. N-S-I-D-E is supposed to be short for Northside."

"Jenn's right, though. It sorta does look like *inside*!"

Devin joked. "Maybe it will work as a diversion tactic and confuse the other team?"

A couple of the girls laughed. Devin felt pretty happy for the moment. The whole night was buzzing with energy. Despite a few disagreements, she and Chloe had been working together fairly well at practice over the past week, too, and Devin had almost forgotten about the e-mail Leila had showed her. Devin may never have expected to find herself in this position, standing in front of all these people and wearing a Northside cheerleading uniform, but she was glad that she was there now. And she was glad that all her hard work at gymnastics was paying off.

Lately Devin had realized she was yearning for her old life less and less. Cheerleading kept her busy, and it was a great distraction from missing home. Josh hadn't completely come around to the idea of the "new Devin," but at least the two of them were relatively back to normal again. He'd even video chatted with her right before she left for the game this evening, just to wish her luck.

Most of the girls had taken extra time getting ready for homecoming, so everyone's makeup was more elaborate than usual. They'd even tested out their new competition hairstyle: a diagonal French braid framing the left side of the face, then pulled back into a low, sleek ponytail and finished off with a crisp white cheer bow. Carley had volunteered to paint each JV squad member's graduation year on her bow with glitter puff paint. It looked so adorable that the Varsity girls asked her to do theirs, too.

Devin felt bright and shiny as she waved to her mom and Sage. The two of them sat up in the bleachers near a poster that said CRUSH ELLIOT HIGH!, chomping on hot dogs from the Wolf Pack Snack Shack. It was the first time Sage had come to a game to watch Devin cheer. Sage stood and motioned to Devin that she was going to come down and say hi before the game started.

Kate looked up to the stands. "Is that your sister?"

"Yup, that's her." Devin sighed, looking up at the stands. Sage looked exactly like Devin, only a little more refined and a few years older. She bounced down the stairs of the bleachers, with her red hair tied up in a ponytail and wearing one of Linda's new NHS sweatshirts.

"Hey, kid!" Sage grabbed her little sister and enveloped her in a tight hug. "Never thought I'd see you like this!" Sage pinched the fabric of Devin's blue sleeve. "What was that thing you said to me a few months ago?"

"Cheerleading is for shallow idiots?" Devin cringed.

"Oh yeah! Wasn't there a song about it, too?" Sage laughed and pushed Devin's shoulder. "You little jerk! I think it went something like—"

"No, no! Don't sing it here." Devin began to laugh, recalling the dumb song she and Josh had made up one afternoon for the sole purpose of teasing Sage. "I don't think my new teammates would appreciate its subtle humor."

"Okay, okay..." Sage glanced behind her sister at the rest of the squad. Chloe was watching the sisters' interaction intently. She seemed curious about Sage, the girl who'd helped secure Devin a position on the squad. "Is that your cocaptain? The pretty blond one up front?"

"How did you guess?" Devin replied under her breath.

"She has that look about her—like the world is on her shoulders. I've seen it before." Sage pointed to herself. "Actually, I lived it."

Devin looked back at Chloe, who was now helping Jenn stretch by sitting across from her in straddle position on the grass. They held hands and took turns leaning forward and then back again.

"Well, the only thing that's on her shoulders is usually Emily or Arianna during a shoulder sit. It's one of the few stunts she wants to do on a regular basis. Isn't that lame?" Devin sighed. "It's so frustrating! I have all these great ideas about new stunts and tumbles we can try, and she never wants to do them. I think she's afraid of someone getting hurt. She almost never respects that I am supposed to have a say in things, too."

Sage leaned against the bleacher railing and crossed her arms over her chest. "Well, maybe she's right, Dev."

"What?" Devin turned to her sister in disbelief. "Are

you sticking up for Chloe over *me*?" Devin suddenly felt more dull than shiny. Her sister always knew the exact thing to say to bring her back down to earth. It was usually a good thing, but sometimes it hurt.

"Sorry, Dev, but I think I am." Sage smiled, not so sympathetically. What sort of look was that? Was Sage in on some plan with Coach Steele to teach Devin a lesson about compromise?

"But she has been so hard on me! All I'm trying to do is fit in here and with this team—why can't she see I'm only trying to help? It's not my fault that I got elected as a captain, too!" Devin said.

"I think you need to put yourself in her position. You came in out of nowhere and stole her captainship. That must be hard," Sage reminded Devin.

Devin hated it when her sister did this. They had only said hello a few minutes ago and Devin was already getting a lecture about something she'd done wrong. Sage didn't know the whole story, so it wasn't even a fair assessment. She didn't know about the wicked, backstabbing e-mail. "I only did this for Mom, you know. And I'm trying my best," Devin replied curtly before running back over to join her teammates.

"Well, try harder!" Sage called out, drawing a few wayward glances from parents who probably thought she might be some sort of young stage mother. "Go, sis!" she added quickly before jogging back up the bleachers to watch the game.

Coach Steele blew her whistle and motioned for the girls to huddle up for the pregame pep talk. But instead of jogging over, Devin launched her body into a back handspring. The crowd clapped and she waved up at them. "GO, NORTHSIDE!" she yelled. She would show Sage just how great a cheerleader she was without her help.

"You're not supposed to be tumbling on the concrete, Devin," Chloe said. "You know that." She crossed her arms over her chest, expecting Devin to argue.

"Whoops, sorry," Devin replied. She actually had forgotten that rule momentarily but didn't want to admit it. "You're right, Chloe."

Chloe looked a little taken aback that Devin was agreeing with her again. Maybe she was feeling the team spirit.

"Huddle up, girls!" Coach instructed, and they all gathered together. Devin was squashed uncomfortably between Marcy and Leila. "The day has finally come. It's homecoming! Today, we are going to show Elliot High what Northside can do. We know the football team is going to give it everything they have, and it goes without saying that each of you will, too. Give those fans in the stands a show! Give them something to cheer for! I want to see sharp motions, big smiles, and high jumps. I want to hear your voices from the other side of the field. I want to hear them from Africa. I want to hear them from MARS. Give those Tar Heels a preview of what they will be up against at competition. But most of all, the most important thing I want you girls to remember is..."

Coach Steele took a deep breath and looked down at the ground. She popped her head back up, grinning. "...HAVE FUN!"

"Coach, that was super-cheese," Emily said with a laugh. "But I was into it."

"Thanks, Emily. Any other words from our captains?" Coach Steele looked to Devin and then over to Chloe. The two girls exchanged a look that seemed to signal a temporary truce. "It's not whether you win or lose..." said Devin.

"It's how loud you CHEER!" continued Chloe.

"Ah, they finally learn!" Coach Steele shouted.

All of them put their hands in the center and shouted "N-H-S!" as they released their arms out from the huddle like a firework. And for once, the fireworks continued. For the first time in years, Northside High won its homecoming game. Granted, it was by one point. But that was all it took. The JV Timberwolves couldn't help hoping that the same good luck would carry them all the way to Regionals.

CHAPTER 20

Chloe was wearing a royal-blue minidress with a scooped neckline and a low back. It was a little more revealing than she was used to, but it was a big night, and her first high school homecoming dance seemed like the perfect opportunity to blow off some steam and not worry about routines or homework for a few hours.

The thrill of winning the game hadn't yet worn off, and everyone was feeling the Northside High spirit. Blue was definitely the right choice for the captain of the JV cheerleading team.

Chloe admired her dress in the mirror and went to work on her hair. She picked up a curling iron and began to twirl small sections of hair around the barrel to create a dramatic, old-Hollywood wave. There were also three flatirons plugged into the outlet above Chloe's bathroom counter.

"Isn't that a bit overkill, you guys?" Devin asked, watching as Chloe smoothed down a perfect blond curl.

"No," Chloe replied. "They're all for different purposes. See?" She fluffed her hair out to illustrate her point.

"Totally," said Emily, leaning forward into the mirror to glue a set of false eyelashes to her lids. "Aren't these great?" she said, batting them.

"If you want to look like a Muppet!" Kate teased, picking up the package and inspecting it. "Good for multiple uses," Kate read from the box. "You could wear them at competition, Em."

"Maybe I will," Emily huffed, and snatched it back. "Go, Muppets!"

Devin crossed over to the mirror. She was wearing a short black dress with a silk bodice and a pleated chiffon skirt. Her eye makeup was smoky, and Emily had convinced her to wear a bold shade of red lipstick. Even Chloe had to admit that Devin looked really pretty.

"Thanks for inviting me, Chloe," Devin said, studying Chloe's face in the mirror. Devin still didn't understand how this could be the same girl who'd written that mean e-mail to everyone about her.

"Of course," Chloe replied. At the end of the game last

night, Chloe had invited Devin to get ready for the dance with her, Kate, and Emily. Maybe she was on a victory high, or maybe they had finally gotten used to each other. Whatever it was, Chloe was going with it. Butting heads with Devin every day was exhausting and counterproductive. "It only makes sense that we all get ready here anyway, since I'm lucky enough not to share a bathroom," Chloe added, waving her hand from the en suite bathroom into her bedroom.

"You really have no idea how lucky you are, Chloe." Kate sighed. Sharing with three little kids was disgusting, to say the least.

Devin sat down on a gold chair in Chloe's room and looked around. She was impressed by the Davises' home. When her mom had dropped Devin off at the enormous house, the two of them had double-checked the address, just to be sure they had the right one. It was a classic design—two stories high, with white Roman columns near the entry and strategic landscaping that provided a sense of privacy. A kitschy mailbox out front with three painted wooden cheerleaders (two girls and a boy) on top was the only true sign of character.

The inside of the house was just as lavish as the exterior. Cushy couches in rich fabrics sat in the living room, and a vast Persian rug lay on the shiny parquet floor. It was a far cry from the peeling wallpaper at Devin's new house.

"Can I use one of those?" Devin asked before crossing over to the bathroom counter and picking up one of the flatirons.

"Sure." Chloe nodded in response, and Devin began to attack one of her red curls with the tool.

"That's going to take such a long time," Kate said, watching Devin struggle with a small piece of her hair. "Let me help you." She picked up a fat red curl and one of the other flatirons and went to work. Soon Emily had joined in as well, and the girls competed to see how fast they could straighten Devin's hair. It was harder than it sounded.

"You look hot!" Emily cooed at the sight of the new, sleek Devin Isle.

Devin smiled as she looked at her reflection, and then suddenly felt sad. "It's a pity it's sort of a waste," she said, thinking of Josh. Just as she had suspected, Josh had told her it would be way too hard for him to come down to the dance. But Devin felt sad about more than that. She was finally realizing that he would never be able to go with her to *any* dances, not just this one. It was a hard reality for the two of them to face.

"You guys ready?" Chloe asked, impatient to get to the dance and start having a great time. Emily, Kate, and Devin nodded. They were all nervous for completely different reasons.

Once they'd snapped a few pictures and were squished into Mr. Davis's car, Devin turned the group's attention to Emily and her impending musical debut. "What time do you go on?" Devin asked. She was excited to hear Emily sing with Hashtag, especially since it was all Emily had talked about for weeks during breaks at practice.

"Around nine, I think," Emily said. Her voice sounded a little shakier than normal. "I'm so glad I don't have a date right now. I have no idea how I'd deal with that *and* freaking out about this show! Eeeeep!" Emily squealed, and then smiled.

"Well, you look superhot." Chloe smiled. "I doubt you'll have any trouble finding a boy to dance with when you're not onstage singing."

"Maybe Dean?" Emily giggled. "Man, he is so cute."

"What about that guy from the band? Travis?" Devin said, attempting to involve herself in the conversation. She was finally getting better at remembering who everyone at school was.

Emily turned to Devin. "What about Travis?"

"He likes you, right?" Devin replied. "I mean, that's what I heard...."

"From who?" Emily lapped up the information hungrily. "Was it Brandon?"

Devin laughed. "I don't know. Some guy in the hallway by my locker yesterday. Could have been a Brandon."

"Interesting…" Emily said, and began to stare out the window to reflect on this new tidbit. "Hey, Kate—what's going on with the junior guy from English? I still think you're crazy for telling him no."

Devin felt Kate instantly stiffen beside her. "Nothing's going on with him. We aren't right for each other anyway."

"Why do you say that?" Chloe asked, looking into the side mirror from the front seat.

"He makes me too nervous," Kate admitted. "It's scary."

"So does performing at competition, but it's worth it!" Chloe said with a smile.

"Well, I will just be excited for that, then!" Kate replied. "Cheerleading is life, right, Chloe?"

"Good point," Chloe said, laughing.

Kate stared out the window, feeling a sense of dread wash over her. She had never actually responded to Adam's sweet Shakespearean note. Instead, she'd acted like a complete chicken and ignored it altogether. Every day in class, they would talk about the assignments. Whenever Adam sounded like he was about to bring it up, Kate would quickly change the subject. Then, when the bell rang, she would dart right out of the classroom. It was humiliating. How could she spend hours performing in front of a giant crowd and then choke on a simple conversation with a boy who liked her?

He wouldn't have understood anyway. In Kate's mind,

not going with him was the right thing to do because she'd just ruin it. Too bad she didn't actually have the guts to tell him that. By now Adam probably thought she hated him. Kate wondered if she'd run into him at the dance. Or worse, see him there with another girl. She pushed the thought from her mind and decided to just deal with it when the time came.

"You girls have fun!" Mr. Davis said as they exited the car. Chloe felt weird wearing such a fancy outfit to the same place where she normally wore sweats, but as soon they walked into the gym, the sense that they were at school melted away completely. Emily and the dance committee had done an incredible job transforming the gym into Camelot. Chloe actually felt a little like she was stepping into a medieval castle, or at least a really pretty Renaissance faire, rather than a stinky sports facility.

The dance floor was in the center of the room, roped off with gold cord and tassels, while the surrounding areas were divided with yards of a sheer silver fabric printed to look like stones. As promised, a huge inflatable dragon attacked the DJ booth with orange and red streamers made to look like fire hanging from its mouth. A life-sized suit of armor greeted the guests at the door, and the disco ball hanging from the ceiling cast hundreds of tiny reflections across the basketball court and onto every possible surface.

"So what do you guys think?" said Emily, gazing at her handiwork proudly.

"This is so surreal!" shouted Devin, walking farther inside and doing a little spin to try it out. She had been dreading the dance a bit, but now that she was all dressed up and standing there, she felt excited about the rest of the night. The song transitioned into the new Katy Perry single. "Come on, Kate! Come dance with me!"

"Um, okay!" Kate shouted over the loud music. She couldn't help herself from scanning the room to look for any sign of Adam in the animated crowd. But the combination of low lighting and loud music made it nearly impossible to recognize anyone. Kate let herself get pulled into the mass of dancing teenagers, reaching out for Chloe's arm and dragging her along as well. Emily had already disappeared somewhere because she was sort of "on duty" all night as a homecoming committee member and the singer in the band.

The three girls twirled and bounced along to the beat, throwing their arms in the air. For once, they didn't have to worry if their elbows were perfectly locked in place. It was all about feeling the music and just having fun.

"Hey, guys! Over here!" Jenn and Carley shouted from a corner of the dance floor. They had staked out a spot right next to the DJ booth so they could request songs. Jenn was wearing a purple halter dress and an elaborate jeweled headband across her blond hair, which fell down in soft curls onto her shoulders. Her nails were done in a French manicure just for the dance, too.

"Nice nails!" Devin shouted over the music.

"Thanks! It sucks that I have to take the polish and tips off after tonight, but I love the way they look!" She waved her hands around like a magician. "Sometimes I wish we didn't have to keep our nails short for cheerleading," Jenn lamented before starting up a sexy hip move to the beat again.

"Great dress, Chloe!" Carley shouted. "You look super-hot tonight."

"Thanks. So do you! Love the red! You kind of look like a brunette Taylor Swift," Chloe said. Carley was wearing a strapless crimson minidress. Her long brown hair fell sleek and straight around her face and down her back.

"Really?" Carley squealed. "That's what I was going for!" Chloe smiled at Carley's genuine excitement and took in the atmosphere of the dance. Everyone seemed to be having such a great time, all dressed up and hanging out together in the gorgeous gym. She breathed a huge sigh of relief. This was just what the team needed.

Leila and Marcy walked up to them wearing a couple of very short dresses and fake smiles. "Hey, Captain!" Leila exclaimed. "Looking good, Chloe." Her eyes darted across to Devin and then back to Chloe again. "Did you guys get ready together?"

"Yeah! We went to Chloe's house! It was awesome," Devin replied. She wanted Leila to know that she and Chloe were getting along. She just wanted to put the past, and that e-mail, behind them. "Hey, I'm gonna go and grab a soda really fast. I'm already thirsty! Do you guys want one?"

"No, thanks!" Leila yelled, smiling.

"I'm all set!" Chloe shouted over the music.

Leila waited until Devin was out of sight and then turned to Chloe. "So, are you two, like, *friends* now?"

"Well, I don't know about that, but it's getting there!" Chloe replied. She began dancing again. She didn't understand where this conversation was going. But Leila clearly had something to get off her chest.

"It just seems weird, you know!" Leila shouted. "The way she talks about you to the other girls! I neeeever thought you guys would get along."

"What are you talking about?" Chloe shot back. Leila had caught her attention.

"Devin is always telling everyone what a tyrant you are. She walks around saying this stuff all the time. She thinks you're totally stale and boring and never want to try anything new. I'm surprised you haven't heard her yourself. Anyway, she, like, teaches everyone the stuff you don't want us to do!" Leila stopped dancing. "You know, because she's the captain, too! So she can."

"She really said all those things about me?" Chloe asked. She usually dismissed what Leila said as nonsense, but Chloe wasn't so sure this time. It actually made sense. How else would everyone have voted for Devin as captain only days after joining the squad if she wasn't undermining Chloe's ideas behind her back?

But still, the source this was coming from was unreliable. "How am I supposed to believe you, Leila?" Chloe said over the music.

"Duh, I'm one of your oldest childhood friends!" Leila exclaimed. "Why would I lie to you?" Leila made the most innocent face she could muster. "I just wouldn't!"

Chloe wasn't so sure about that.

An hour later, Kate was feeling a little danced out and bored. She was disappointed that she hadn't seen Adam anywhere yet. Kate assumed that meant he hadn't even come to the dance—maybe because of her. The thought made her feel sad and guilty.

Kate stepped outside into the cool fall evening to take a breather. Emily and Hashtag were setting up their equipment on the little platform at the front of the gym. They'd be going on in about ten minutes, and Kate at least had to stay for that performance before calling her dad for a ride home.

A chilly breeze blew through the air, and Kate's flowy dress did little to shield her from it. Emily had insisted that Kate buy this one, saying the color looked amazing against her dark skin, but Kate now wished she'd chosen a dress with a little more substance. She shivered and wrapped her arms around her body, then took a seat on one of the benches. There were a few kids from the dance wandering around the dark quad, goofing off. Another couple stood under a nearby tree, making out.

"Hey, Kate," said a voice behind her. Kate turned around to see Adam approaching. He was wearing black pants and a blue dress shirt and looked like he'd even added a little bit of gel to his unruly hair.

"Oh, hey," she said. Her voice was shaky. "You're here!"

"I know—it's surprising, isn't it? After surviving the rejection of the century and everything!" Adam smiled and walked closer so that he was standing directly in front of her. "That really burned, Cheer Girl."

"What are you talking about?" Kate said. But she knew exactly what he was talking about.

"You got my note. I saw you reading it," Adam said, deflated. "You could have told me, you know."

"Told you what?" Kate asked, feeling suddenly desperate to explain herself.

"That you weren't into dudes who do back tucks," Adam joked. "I would have understood."

Kate laughed nervously. She shook her head in protest. "But that's not true at all! I really wanted to go with you. I was just...scared."

"Of me?" Adam said, laughing. "Are you serious, Kate?"

"Is that dumb?" Kate asked, beginning to smile as well. Adam was right; he wasn't intimidating in the slightest. He was just a nice guy who liked her. Who happened to have some mysterious talents. And she liked him back. "I wish I hadn't messed up the chance to go to the dance with you."

"You didn't!" Adam grabbed her hands and put them on his shoulders. "Look! We're at the dance." He put his hands around her waist. Kate giggled.

"And listen to that—it's a slow song." Adam twirled her around and pulled her in close. "So let's dance."

Kate allowed herself to lean on Adam's shoulder and close her eyes. They swayed to the music and she tried hard to concentrate on anything besides the fact that her heart was doing double time in her chest. When the song was over, Adam leaned back and looked her in the eye.

"Adam?" Kate said.

"Yes, Lady Kate?"

"Where did you learn to do a standing back tuck?" she asked, smiling.

"Ah. That, my fair maiden, I cannot reveal," Adam said, smirking back at her. "Why? Were you impressed?"

"Yes, but—"

Before Kate even had the chance to say anything more, Adam leaned in and kissed her. She melted into him, completely lost in the moment. Kate had never experienced a real kiss like this one before.

They pulled apart. Another breeze blew through and Kate shivered. She looked over Adam's shoulder toward the gym and saw that Devin had wandered outside and witnessed the entire thing. Devin gave Kate a little wave and a quick thumbs-up. She mimed zipping up her lips before heading back inside. But keeping Adam a secret from the other girls suddenly didn't matter so much to Kate.

"I'm glad that you were impressed," Adam continued. "It means my plan worked."

"Well, not entirely." Kate giggled. "I didn't come to the dance with you."

"Thanks for reminding me," Adam replied, miming an arrow being shot straight through his heart. "Want to head inside? More dancing awaits in there...." Adam said, gesturing awkwardly to the gym.

"I would love that," replied Kate. She was still reeling from that kiss.

As the two of them wandered into the gym to catch

Hashtag's first song, Adam reached for Kate's hand and squeezed it. "This band is surprisingly in tune," he said, grinning.

"Yeah, that's my best friend, Emily, the singer!" Kate added, looking up at her friend in admiration. Emily was belting out a long note, and a spotlight shone down on her. The moment the song ended, the dance floor erupted in cheers. As Emily smiled and took a bow, Kate could not remember a moment when she'd been happier.

CHAPTER 21

The kitchen counter in the MacDonald house was covered with peanut butter and chocolate chips. Kate's six-year-old stepbrother, Garrett, smeared it around on the surface as if it were finger paint while her four-year-old stepbrother, Jack, sprinkled more chocolate chips on top to "help." Kate didn't mind the mess they were making, because it was keeping them preoccupied and quiet. She'd learned that little kids were usually being loud, messy, or obnoxious. So, if you only got two out of the three, it was a pretty successful day. She'd just clean up the peanut butter later.

Luckily, her dad and stepmom would be home soon

with the rest of her baking supplies. Then she could hurry up and finish making her batches of peanut butter fudge brownies for the cheerleading bake sale that afternoon. She only had one batch so far, and she'd promised at least three.

Cartoons blared from the family room and her little sister, Sasha, attempted to ride their Australian shepherd, Scout, like a horse down the hallway. Poor Scout whimpered in despair. "Off the doggie, Sash!" Kate yelled. *"Now."* Sasha dismounted the poor dog and pouted her way back to the other room.

Normally, the constant activity in the house made Kate feel manic. But in the week since homecoming—since she and Adam had kissed—not much seemed to bother her. She had never felt like this before. It was as if every problem she had in her life seemed a little easier just by thinking about that one moment at the dance.

Adam and Kate had seen each other in English every day since the dance, but both of them were playing it cool. The way they chatted, mostly about schoolwork, almost made Kate feel like the kiss had never happened. But Kate didn't know what to say or do next. She could tell by the way he looked at her that he was calculating his next move like it was a game of chess. She was so useless at boys. And chess, for that matter.

Standing in the kitchen, Kate thought of how soft his lips were and how her body had felt leaning against him, his arms wrapped around her. She thought of how, for some reason, his neck had smelled like cinnamon. Kate opened up a bottle of ground cinnamon that she already had out on the counter and let the scent linger for a moment. What a random cologne for a boy to have.

The doorbell rang, lifting Kate from her daydream.

"I'll get it!" Sasha screeched, running to the front door. Jack and Garrett soon followed, hands completely covered in chocolate and peanut butter. "I'll get it! I'll get it!" they yelled. Scout began barking.

"Sasha, get Scout to stop barking right now!" Kate yelled.

"Scouty, no bark! Bad dog!" Sasha tried to climb on Scout again, and the dog took off down the hallway to hide in a back room.

Kate hoped the kids hadn't scared off whoever had rung the doorbell, but when she reached the front step, no one was there. All she saw was a beat-up red Volvo driving off down the street. Kate jogged her memory but didn't recognize the car at all. *Oh well*, she thought.

"Hey! A present!" Garrett shouted, plucking something off the front step. He wrapped his dirty, slimy hand around a small piece of paper tied up like a scroll. It was tied with a blue-and-silver ribbon....

Had Adam seriously just driven to her house? And heard all the shouting? No wonder he ran away!

"That's for Katey, Garrett! Please give it to me...." Kate said as she carefully removed the letter from his little hand like it was a shaky Jenga block, ready to topple the tower at any second. If done incorrectly, taking something from a little kid could end very badly. He looked like he was about to erupt in tears, but luckily Kate's parents arrived home at that same moment. All it took was a new distraction and she was free with her prize. She hightailed it to the only place in the house where she could count on being alone.

The warm dryer rumbled and shook underneath Kate as she sat on the edge. It was one of the few places she could sit without her long legs touching the floor, so she liked to swing them around. The scroll was covered in peanut butter. Kate did her best to wipe it off with a nearby sock before unfurling it to read the text. All it said was:

Kate,
"our doubts are traitors."
Blackberry Hill Park, 1 pm
—Adam
P.S. Should I still be doing this? or is it lame now? whatever, I'm going with it.

The last part especially made Kate smile. The whole note thing was sort of charming. But what was he trying to say with that quote? Kate knew she recognized it from a play by Shakespeare, but she didn't really know what it had to do with the two of them. Maybe he was having doubts or second thoughts about having kissed her!

Kate looked at the clock on the wall. It was 12:47. If she rode her bike, she could get to Blackberry Hill Park by 1:00 PM easily. And the bake sale wasn't until three, so she had plenty of time to come back home and finish everything before then. Kate had to go. She sneaked out the back door, grabbed her blue Schwinn from the garage, and headed off toward the park.

❋

"I didn't mean to weird you out with those notes, Cheer Girl," Adam said to Kate as they sat next to each other on the playground swings. He was looking especially cute, wearing some old jeans, a T-shirt with a disco-dancing astronaut on it, and his usual horn-rimmed glasses. Adam's legs were way longer than those of the average kid who used the swing, so his knees pointed up to the sky. He pushed himself back and forth while keeping his feet flat on the ground. "Did I? Weird you out, I mean."

"No, of course not," Kate replied, and laughed nervously. "Honestly, it weirds me out more when you call me Cheer Girl." *What a lame attempt at a joke*, she thought. Kate stared down at her feet on the sand below, unable to look him in the eye.

"Really?" Adam replied. He sounded disappointed. "Way to go, dumb ass!" he said to himself. "I thought you sorta liked it." He looked up at her. "I mean, I hope you know I've been kidding this whole time about the whole cheerleaders-being-ditzy thing. I know it's just a cliché."

"I figured...once I saw you do that trick during the rally," Kate replied, attempting another laugh. "Admit it, you are a secret cheerleader...or maybe a ninja?" She fiddled with the hem of her yellow floral sundress. The mood between them was a bit awkward—nothing like it had been on the magical homecoming night, which she'd been thinking about for days on end. Kate couldn't figure out where things had gone wrong.

"I wish," said Adam. He pushed his glasses higher onto the bridge of his nose. "Unfortunately, the actual story is not *that* interesting. My sister taught me one summer. She coaches youth gymnastics, and I was her 'example' of an absolute beginner," Adam confessed. "I fell on my head a lot. But I helped some kids feel better about themselves!"

"It's sort of cool that you can do one," Kate said, lifting her feet off the ground and attempting to swing. "Back tucks are really hard. Half the girls on my squad are still trying to get theirs right. Yours is actually even better than mine, I think."

"It's a great party trick," replied Adam. He lifted his legs and tried to start swinging, too. They were silent for a moment.

"So why have you been avoiding me?" Kate finally asked, surprised at her own courage. Once she started talking, she couldn't stop herself. "And what was the quote from Shakespeare supposed to mean? Are you having doubts about ever liking me now?"

"What? Haven't *you* been avoiding *me*?" Adam asked, standing up. The swing rocked back and forth once released from his weight.

"What? Of course I haven't! I have been talking to you in class every day!" Kate stood up to face him. "Didn't you know that was me trying to tell you how I feel about you?"

"By discussing last night's assigned reading?" Adam replied. He was now grinning widely. "That's your big trademark move, Cheer Girl? In-depth discussions of the latest homework?"

"Well, yeah." Kate shrugged. "How else am I supposed to do it? You used a Shakespeare quote!"

"But that's Shakespeare! That's, like, designed for romance. Has anyone ever told you that you aren't the best communicator?" Adam teased.

Kate scoffed at the silly notion. First of all, he'd hardly chose the most romantic plays. Second of all, she'd never received anything lower than an A on her written essays. So of course she was a good communicator. Also, she spent every single Friday night yelling words at a crowd of people. "No way! Never."

"Well, I am. Right now." Adam laughed and took a couple steps closer. "Kate MacDonald, you are really cute, but you suck at talking to guys." He put his hands on her waist and slowly pulled her to him. Kate let herself relax. "Even nerdy ones like me."

Their lips touched again.

The kiss lasted longer this time, but it was just as satisfying as the first time, at the dance. Kate shivered. Her nerves were working overtime.

"So what was the quote supposed to mean, then?" she asked, finally feeling confident enough to look him in the eye again.

Adam shrugged. "I guess I was just trying to tell you to let go of some of your doubts. If you had any about me."

"Oh." Kate blushed. "I guess I was just nervous."

Adam smiled. "Me too." He gestured to the swings. "So why don't we just 'hang out' for now and see where it goes? No pressure."

"Did you seriously just make that pun?" Kate couldn't help but laugh at his complete and utter geekiness.

"Yes. Is it a deal breaker?" he asked, plopping back down in the swing.

"Not at all."

CHAPTER 22

It was a gorgeous day to be outside, so Emily didn't mind that she had to spend her Saturday afternoon setting up the Northside cheerleading team bake sale. The Sunny Valley Farmers' Market had booths selling all sorts of delicious fruits and veggies from local organic farms. There were also booths selling fresh cheeses and baguettes from Le Parisien Bakery, and a few dedicated entirely to flowers and gardening supplies.

The NHS booth was in a prime spot by the exit of the market. Emily had chosen it specifically because she knew how shoppers worked: if you had a booth right at the entrance, no one would buy anything because they would want to wait and view all of their options first. The middle was bad because people would finally be in the mood to buy—but usually only the healthy items that they had come for. By the time customers reached the exit, they would be ready to splurge on one more treat before heading home. It was perfect. Emily couldn't wait to blow the last fund-raiser's record out of the water. If they earned enough, they wouldn't have to raise more money until after the Regional competition *and* they'd be able to donate to their charity cause, Hearts Heal. Sometimes, helping out the community made Emily feel even better than cheering at games. It didn't look bad on college applications, either.

"Hey, Em! Where do the cupcakes go?" Marcy Martinez said, walking up to the booth in her gold NHS CHEERLEADERS T-shirt and blue camp shorts. She had worn her white ribbon in her ponytail, as instructed. If there was anything Emily had learned about cheerleading fund-raisers from all of her family's years as NHS supporters, it was that people expected to see them looking like cheerleaders. Something about wearing bows in their hair and smiles on their faces always seemed to do the trick.

"Cupcakes on the main table right here, since there are a bazillion of them," Emily said, wishing she'd assigned people treats instead of letting them choose their own. At least cupcakes were trendy right now. So far they had red velvet, vanilla, chocolate, rainbow confetti, and coconut cream, and Devin had brought three strawberry-rhubarb pies, which people had already started dishing out.

"Where is Kate with those peanut butter fudge brownies?" Chloe stood up from her seat at the cash box and scanned the park. "She's never late, and I've been waiting to eat one of those first!"

"Chloe, the baked goods are not for us—they are for *sale*," Emily warned her friend. This event was Emily's baby, and she would not have it ruined by Chloe's sweet tooth. "We have to sell them or else we won't make the fees for Regionals."

"Oh, don't you worry, Em. I'll pay for what I eat." Chloe gave in and chose a red velvet cupcake with the letters *NHS* iced on top.

Two hours later, the booth was still going strong. Even more squad members had brought baked goods, replenishing their resources for the time being. Chloe had done a round through the market, passing out flyers that directed people to their booth, but now she was getting tired. She sat down next to Emily at the table.

"I haven't seen Kate yet, have you?" Chloe had been so

distracted that she'd forgotten to keep an eye out for her best friend. Chloe clicked on her cell to check the time and noticed it was almost five o'clock. Kate, the girl who panicked when she was only five minutes early to class, was late by two hours. She scrolled through her contacts and selected Kate's name. The phone rang once and then went directly to her voice-mail message. "Hi, it's Kate." Her voice sounded tiny and robotic. "Please leave me a message, because it's nice. But text me if you need me right away!"

Chloe clicked off the phone and looked out into the crowd. She looked for little kids running around. Whenever the MacDonald family traveled as a pack, there was always a flurry of activity surrounding them. Kate's three younger siblings, Jack, Garrett, and Sasha, were a handful. Chloe smoothed her golden bangs, which she'd chosen to leave out of her ponytail today, and took a seat next to Emily at the table. Chloe composed a short text to Kate and hoped she would get a reply fast. She was actually starting to get concerned.

"Has Kate seemed weird to you lately?" Chloe asked, selecting a second cupcake and taking a large bite from it. A bit of cream cheese icing clung to her lip, and she licked it off shamelessly. Chloe could eat sweets all day long and be completely satisfied. "First, she forgot the words and moves to a really easy cheer during a football game, and then she disappeared for a while at the homecoming dance. And now she's late to the bake sale? By two whole hours? It's just so un-Kate!" Chloe threw the cupcake wrapper in the trash and leaned back in her folding chair.

"I guess she has been acting a little bit shady," Emily replied, counting out one-dollar bills and putting them back in the cash box. Someone called her name and Emily turned and waved, flashing a huge toothy smile but still talking to Chloe at the same time. "What do you think it is?"

"Well..." Chloe wiped her mouth with one of the royal-blue napkins that Emily had stocked up on before the fund-raiser. "I have an idea. I think she has been secretly seeing that guy, the junior!" It came out as a bit accusatory.

"It's possible, but so what if she is? More power to her, I say." Emily sighed, clearly not invested in having this conversation at the moment. "Or, I don't know, maybe it's just that she has too much homework. She is in all those advanced classes."

Chloe hadn't really considered that, but it was true. Kate did have a lot going on with all those classes. Emily did, too. She'd just planned the entire homecoming dance *and* performed at it. Now she was running the whole bake sale! It suddenly dawned on Chloe how preoccupied she'd been lately with trying to compete against Devin all the time. She hadn't even noticed her friends struggling, too. Right now, Emily looked like she was about to crack. She had dark circles under her eyes, and her normally perfect skin was starting to break out.

"Do you need me to help with anything?" Chloe asked Emily.

"Actually, that would be great!" Emily replied. "I know you're gonna hate this, but can you and Devin go across the street to the supermarket and buy a couple more cases of bottled water? We're completely out, and we really need it for the coolers."

"Totally," said Chloe with a smile. She got up to go find Devin. This would be interesting. Chloe hadn't been able to shake what Leila had told her at the dance about Devin talking about her behind her back. Chloe soon found Devin smelling some bouquets of flowers in a nearby stall. Chloe tried to make a joke. "You stopping to smell the roses?"

"Hydrangeas, actually," Devin replied awkwardly.

Whenever the two of them talked by themselves, it felt a little forced. While it had looked like things were going well between Chloe and Devin before the dance, they went downhill again right afterward. But Chloe felt that it wasn't one-sided. Devin clearly still had some issues with Chloe that she needed to work out as well.

"Emily wants us to go get more cases of water," Chloe said, getting to the point.

"All right," Devin answered, and the two of them headed toward the store. They walked in silence.

"Have you seen Kate anywhere?" Chloe asked, though she doubted Devin of all people would have more information than she did. "I texted her, but she never wrote back. I'm a little worried. The bake sale is almost over...."

"Oh, she's fine. But she's not coming," Devin said, like it was no big deal. "She texted me. Something about a flat tire on her bike and being stuck in Blackberry Hill Park."

Chloe couldn't believe her ears. "Kate texted *you*?"

"Yeah, she said not to worry," Devin replied. "What's the problem now?"

Chloe didn't know how to respond to this new information: her best friend, Kate, had chosen to text Devin over *her*. How was it possible that she trusted Devin more? Chloe and Kate had grown up together, cheered together as kids, and now were finally on the Northside team together. This was not how things were supposed to turn out!

For the next ten minutes, while they were purchasing the water and carrying it back, Chloe tried to come up with a way to end this weird jealous rivalry between the two of them. Chloe felt that Devin needed to be reminded who had actually worked hard to get this status. There had to be a fair way to decide once and for all who deserved to be captain of the JV team.

Then Chloe had a brilliant idea.

"Devin, you know how you really wanted to try a full up in the competition routine?" Chloe asked as she and Devin started to empty the cases of water into some coolers.

"Yeah?" Devin answered, confused at Chloe's sudden enthusiasm for talking to her.

"I think you should do it," Chloe said.

"You do?" Devin was really baffled now. "But I thought you said—"

"I think that we should *both* choreograph a routine for Regionals."

Devin failed to comprehend how they were going to perform two routines at Regionals. "That's never going to work."

"We won't compete with both routines. It's just a way to see who is actually better at being captain," Chloe said. "We'll have the squad vote on which one they like best. If I win, you'll step down. And if you win, I'll step down."

Devin dropped three bottles into the cooler's ice water as she shook her head. "But, Chloe, I never wanted to push you out—"

"Deal?" Chloe cut her off and stuck her hand out for a

shake. Chloe obviously wasn't going to take no for an answer, but Devin had a bad feeling about this. Maybe it was Chloe's opportunity to get what she'd wanted all along—Devin off the JV cheerleading team and out of her way once and for all.

CHAPTER 23

For the most part, everyone on the team had been really into the idea of a cocaptain routine challenge. Coach Steele was its biggest supporter—impressed that the two had finally figured out a healthy, productive way to showcase their different strengths during practice. Amazingly, the challenge did more to promote the two girls getting along than anything else had.

A lot of the other team members had started to fall into a midseason slump, but the new routines reignited a sense of competition and enthusiasm throughout the whole squad. Devin and Chloe strategically forgot to mention to the team that the loser of the unofficial competition would step down as captain. That part was strictly between the two of them. The team just thought it was an inventive way to decide which routine to use at Regionals.

Over the next few weeks, the girls worked extra-hard practicing both of the new routines, which were incredibly different. Chloe's was fast, sharp, and clean, taking few risks beyond the existing skills of the girls. In fact, they had almost perfected it after a few solid practices. Devin's, on the other hand, was a little more ambitious, incorporating some new stunts that they'd never fully hit before, like the tic-tock.

The tic-tock was a complicated arrangement to pull off. The top girl had to stand in a liberty position, and the bases needed to pop with perfect timing. As the bases released the top girl's standing foot, she would switch to her other leg, landing in another liberty, on the opposite leg. Coach Steele insisted that in order to nail that one, they would have to concentrate. They had to want it. Devin certainly did.

Day after day, Coach Steele watched over practice and gave suggestions and corrections, but also tried to step back as much as she could and let the girls work it out themselves. It all seemed like some sort of grand plan to continue helping Chloe and Devin get along, but Chloe also suspected that Coach's behavior was due to her preoccupation with the Varsity team's routine. Winning at Regionals was important to both teams. For the JV girls, it was their only hope to keep the Athletics Boosters funding for the large cheerleading program at Northside. For the seniors on Varsity, it was their last chance to be champions. Jaclyn Downs and Mallory Steiner, the two best cheerleaders on Varsity, were often seen arriving early to their practice and staying late after it ended.

While most of the girls on the JV team were also willing to put in more time and effort, a few of them whined constantly. Marcy was always tired, Arianna had to leave early, and even the normally peppy Kalyn was starting to moan. Everyone seemed to be forgetting about the motto "No pressure, no diamonds." They were beginning to lose their luster.

It was no surprise that Leila, in particular, became a nuisance. Every day after school, she would traipse into practice complaining about a phantom injury or pain. When everyone else was practicing the intense routines full out on the mats, Leila was asking for a water break. And on more than one occasion, Devin had found her hanging outside the bathrooms chatting with some football player and giggling.

It was annoying, but Devin didn't want to confront Leila or get her in trouble with Coach Steele. After Leila had confided in Devin, showing her Chloe's e-mail about kicking Devin off the squad, Devin felt as if she owed Leila something.

Others on the squad had totally stepped up to the plate. Kate had been a bit embarrassed to receive her first demerit—for missing the bake sale—but since then she had been the most dedicated team member. She started showing up at practice five or ten minutes early, trying to prove to someone—Coach Steele or maybe even herself—that she still belonged there and wanted to be on the team. Devin felt kind of bad for Kate, who was punishing herself over one demerit. Still, all the extra work was helping her jumps and tumbling passes improve at a rapid rate.

One afternoon at the end of October, practice had run into overtime. They were supposed to have finished thirty minutes earlier, and everyone was flagging. Devin stood in front of the group with her hands on her hips. "Come on, guys. I know it seems really difficult, but I have seen Sage do this a million times. How hard can it be?" Her old white Hanes T-shirt was patchy with sweat. "Every other squad is going to be doing even harder sequences than this."

"Heel stretches are super-hard for me to do on the ground." Arianna groaned. "Let alone in a pyramid formation." She wiped her forehead with the bottom of her T-shirt, exposing her toned stomach and NHS sports bra.

Kalyn dropped to the floor and nodded in agreement from a straddle position. "Seriously. Can we modify it just a bit?"

Chloe raised her eyebrows and smiled at Devin, like her point had been proven. Devin was about to respond when Jenn piped up. "I know it's taking us longer than we want, but Devin's right. They do look awesome. There's literally no point in going to competition at all if we aren't going to look awesome. Right?"

A couple of the girls nodded.

"Yeah, but what about Elliot and Breckenridge?" Gemma said. She twisted off the cap of her camp water bottle and took a long glug.

"What about them?" Carley asked, tightening her brown hair into a more secure updo.

"Well, they could probably do a stretch pyramid in their sleep," Gemma replied. "This isn't going to impress the judges."

"But just imagine the look on Karen Gelb's face when we hit it," Jenn said, looking far off into the distance. "It will be so worth it."

"And what if we fall? Won't that be worse?" Marcy asked, looking to Leila for backup. "I care more about impressing the judges than the other squads."

"Totally, Marcy," said Chloe. "We shouldn't be pushing it too hard. We should run my routine one more time after this little experiment."

"Experiment?" Devin replied, smiling. "Just you wait, Chloe, we're gonna get it this time."

"Ladies! Move it along!" Coach Steele said, walking over to the group. "Are we socializing or are we stunting?"

"We were just strategizing," said Devin. "But we're totally ready now. Right, girls?" Jenn and Emily clapped and hollered, but the rest of the group was a little reluctant to go again. Practice had now run over by forty minutes. Everyone was thinking about changing out of their gross workout clothes, and what they were going to eat for dinner. Still, they got into position to start the sequence again, for the tenth time in a row.

"Five, six, seven, eight!" Coach Steele shouted as the girls prepared. They positioned themselves in three stunting groups. Devin and Carley stood up front, ready to do their toe touch back tucks. Coach Steele continued, "And one, two..." They locked their bodies in place on the first count, arms tight against their sides. The top girls—Emily, Kalyn, and Lexi—were in the center of each group, prepping themselves to be lifted into the air.

The next step was key as Emily's bases—which consisted of Chloe, Jenn, Marcy, and Kate—lifted her straight into a liberty, one leg bent up like a flamingo. Emily reached out her arms to connect with the two outside groups. She counted the beat and switched legs, sticking the tic-tock. The move was beyond difficult, but she showed no signs of struggle.

Once Emily hit the tic-tock, the outside groups pressed up to heel stretches as Emily came back down to a prep position. The heel stretch pyramid hit for the briefest of moments before Lexi's group lost their hold on her. Lexi's knee buckled and she let her body go, relying on her bases—Leila, Gemma, and Arianna—to catch her safely.

The girls let go of Lexi's foot instantly. If a top girl was going down, one of the worst things to do was to try to force her to stay up by holding on. Every girl on the team knew that was just a twisted ankle waiting to happen.

Even though they hadn't completely hit the stunt, they were definitely getting closer. "Excellent work, guys!" Devin said. "It looked perfect. Other than the end part."

"I knew she was going down. You could see her hips weren't in line at all," said Leila, wringing her wrists dramatically. "And her legs weren't even locked."

"A top girl is only as strong as her weakest base," said Chloe, reciting one of her favorite cheer-campisms. "You do your part and Lexi will do hers."

"Well, I still maintain that I did my part," Leila snapped back. She turned to Lexi and frowned. "It's hardly my fault if my top feels like jelly because she can't lock her knees." Lexi's face fell and she wrapped her arms around her body protectively.

"Out of line, Leila," Coach Steele chided. One of the squad rules was that you didn't comment on each other's form or technique unless what you had to say was constructive. "Maybe you need to do a little strengthening of those arms to provide better support to your teammates."

"But practice is already way past over and I have to go!" Leila whined, pointing to the giant clock on the gym wall.

Coach turned to the entire group. "Everyone give me ten push-ups."

The girls dropped to the mat, but not before shooting Leila a few dirty looks, like she was the kid who had just reminded the teacher to assign homework right before the bell rang. They grunted in unison, using their last bits of energy to complete the set. Coach Steele walked through the lines of girls, inspecting their form.

The Varsity team members, who were waiting patiently on the bleachers for their own practice to start, began to clap and cheer to give the tired JV girls encouragement. "Way to go, Wolves!" they shouted. "N-H-S is the BEST!" The JV girls couldn't help smiling at the support, even though they were tired.

"I want you to run Chloe's routine one more time before you leave," Coach said after they stood up. "Show the Varsity team how it's done!"

The girls quickly got into position, and Coach pressed Play on Chloe's music. Though it involved slightly easier tumbling and stunt sequences, Chloe's routine showed just as many mistakes as Devin's had, which was satisfying for

Devin. Chloe's theory about playing it safe to achieve perfection was completely unfounded. When the music finally ended, the Varsity team cheered for them, and Coach called them all over.

"Good work today, ladies. You all need to go home, rest up, and take an Epsom salts bath for those sore muscles. We have a lot of work still ahead of us. Captains—I'd like a quick word with you." Coach Steele put her right hand in the middle of the circle, and the rest of the team did the same. "N-H-S!" they shouted, lifting their arms above their heads. Then they slumped off to the locker room, leaving Chloe and Devin alone with the coach.

"I just want to make sure everyone is handling learning two routines. It is a lot," she said, raising her eyebrows at the two of them in concern. "You guys are okay, right?"

"Don't worry," said Chloe. "Everyone is really into it. I swear."

"Yeah," Devin added. "And this way we'll already have a second routine to use at Nationals when we win."

"We're still only going to use one routine, even if we win, Devin," Chloe remarked. Devin still didn't know some of the most basic rules about competitive cheerleading.

Coach nodded. "Well, whichever routine we end up with, I want to see you all united as a team, understood?"

Chloe and Devin nodded obediently.

"Good. Now go home and get some rest, because your team is performing at the Varsity game halftime tomorrow!"

"What?" Chloe replied, completely surprised. JV teams never performed during Varsity games. Coach Steele motioned to the bleachers, and Mallory Steiner waved back at them. "The girls thought your team deserved a practice run in front of a packed audience before Regionals, so they agreed to share their slot."

"Wow. That's awesome!" Chloe smiled and held up her hand for a high five with Devin, who held up her hand in response. It was actually a pretty cool opportunity, since the attendance at the JV games had been dwindling as the season wore on.

Devin realized that this was it. They needed to decide which routine to use before the game tomorrow.

"But which routine are we going to do?" Devin asked Coach.

"That's up to you guys," she replied, throwing her hands in the air. "Personally, I think it's time to decide on one anyway. I don't think your squad can handle much more of the double practices."

Neither girl could argue with that statement.

Chloe had an idea as they walked back to the locker room. "I'll set up an anonymous poll on my blog tonight. Then everyone can weigh in on whose routine is better, without us knowing who voted for what! Unlike the e-mail vote for captain." Chloe looked pleased with herself. "I'll e-mail everyone tonight with the link."

"Need me to do anything?" Devin said, although she already knew what the answer would be.

"Nope!" Chloe said cheerily, slinging her bag over her shoulder. "See you tomorrow, Devin. And may the best captain win!" she added before heading out of the locker room doors.

Chloe seemed awfully confident.

As Devin slowly gathered her things, she thought back to the first blog post that Chloe had put up right after the captain announcement at the Medham High game. It had left Devin's name out until the very end, where the cocaptain announcement was thrown in like an afterthought. So it wasn't like Chloe's blog had the best track record for accuracy. It would certainly be interesting to see the results of the so-called anonymous poll.

Congratulations on winning, Chloe, Devin practiced saying in her head as she walked out of the locker room. *You really deserved to win, Chloe.* Even in her thoughts, Devin couldn't make it sound sincere. "I'm stepping down as captain, Chloe," Devin said out loud, to no one. After all, practice made perfect, right?

CHAPTER 24

By the time the football game at Prospect High School rolled around the following evening, almost everyone had voted online for which routine they wanted to perform at the Varsity game and, ultimately, at Regionals. Unfortunately, the decision was split completely down the middle: exactly eight votes for Chloe's routine and eight votes for Devin's. But there were eighteen girls on the squad, so at least two girls hadn't voted, and one more vote was needed to break the tie. No one was coming forward as a holdout.

"All right, give it up, you guys!" Chloe said to the girls before the JV game was about to start. "Who didn't vote?" She was met with a sea of blank faces.

"Honestly, Chloe?" Arianna spoke up, turning to the whole squad. "We all voted. Now raise your hand if you vote to stop voting on things all the time."

Everyone on the squad raised their hands.

"Can't you guys just choose between the two of you and move on? You are like a couple of bickering parents," Leila said, crossing her arms across her chest. "When's the divorce, already?" she added. She looked straight at Devin as she said it.

"Everyone do twenty-five jumping jacks and ten toe touches to warm up," Devin ordered, looking at the whole squad. "Some of you guys haven't even stretched yet, and we only have fifteen minutes to kickoff."

"Oops, did I offend you?" said Leila insincerely. "I'm super-sorry."

It wasn't just that Leila's comment had struck a chord with Devin, who was still touchy about her parents' divorce. The combination of school, the challenge against Chloe, and the less frequent chats with Josh were starting to make Devin feel like everything in her life was spiraling out of control. It was time to stop kidding herself. Why was she doing all of this, again? Pleasing her mother could only go so far, and her mom had yet to book a ticket for Josh to come visit, like she'd promised.

Devin jogged over to her bag and took out a compact mirror. Her hair was done in competition style, a tight

French braid framing the side of her face and pulled back into a low ponytail. Chloe's was done in a traditional high ponytail. In the midst of everything, they had also forgotten to agree on a style for the team to wear to tonight's game. No one matched. Coach was going to call them out on it, for sure.

Nearby, Chloe was interrogating Arianna. "Do you know who it was that didn't vote? How are we supposed to decide, if it's a tie?"

Devin was shocked by Chloe's ability to obsess over the smallest things.

"All right, all right…" Devin said, walking up to them. It was better to just end the whole discussion now. Arianna looked relieved to be released, and scurried off to do warm-up jumps with the rest of the team. "It was me—okay, Chloe? I didn't vote," Devin admitted.

"What? Why not?" Chloe didn't understand. Was she supposed to have not voted as well? They had never said they weren't including themselves. "What, you just decided you wanted to mess up another vote?"

Devin frowned. She wasn't sure what Chloe was implying with that statement.

"I just didn't really feel right about it," said Devin. She was being honest. Last night, after she'd logged on to Chloe's blog, Devin had begun to scroll through all the posts from the season. Chloe had dedicated so much time to each one, posting photos from each game and recapping the highlights, as well as updating everyone on their progress in training for Regionals. There was even a long posting about the bake sale. Devin had always known what cheerleading meant to Chloe, but somehow seeing the proof on the screen like that had made it seem more real. Chloe was so much more of a captain than Devin ever had been. It made her feel bad for bickering with Chloe so much.

So Devin hadn't clicked either box. She was going to let the chips fall where they may, and stay out of the decision.

Chloe rolled her eyes. "Well, I guess congrats on winning, then." Assuming they couldn't figure out who the other missing vote belonged to, it was over. If Chloe deducted her own vote, the score was Chloe 7, Devin 8, and if Devin added in her own vote, the score would be Chloe 8, Devin 9. The math checked out. Devin had bested her and she was the first to admit it, as much as it pained her.

"That's assuming I was going to vote for my own routine," Devin said.

"You weren't?" Chloe replied, confused.

"Not necessarily," said Devin. "You've done a lot of assuming about me this season, Chloe." Devin offered her hand for a shake. "But I vote for you."

"Is this some sort of trick?" Chloe asked. She couldn't understand how Devin's faux-noble act was fitting into her master plan. What was Devin's angle? "First you were all about this challenge, and now you don't even want to fight for your own routine?"

Devin shrugged. "I guess I'm just done with fighting." She gave a sad smile. "You win. After tonight, I'm done with the squad," Devin said, and she walked away to join the rest of the team on the sidelines. As the kickoff buzzer signaled the start of the game, Chloe tried to relish her personal victory over Devin. She was finally going to be the sole captain of the team. It was what Chloe had wanted all year. So why didn't she feel happy?

Later, during their big Varsity halftime debut, they performed Chloe's routine to the huge crowd of Northside fans. It would have gone perfectly if it weren't for one member of the squad who kept messing up the cheers and forgetting the moves. Though it was hard to believe, no one had ever seen the famous Chloe Davis so far off her game.

CHAPTER 25

The whole car ride home from Prospect High had been agonizing, listening to her mother rave about their halftime performance and the upcoming Regionals. Devin didn't have the heart to break it to her mom that she'd quit. There had been enough drama for one night. The last thing Devin needed was a long discussion in which Linda tried to persuade her to reconsider yet again.

As soon she walked through the door of her house, Devin ran to her room and wriggled out of her Northside uniform. It felt like it was suffocating her. She tossed it onto her bedroom floor carelessly. Normally, she'd make some sort of effort at hanging it up so it didn't crease, but it didn't matter now. Pulling on comfy lounge pants and an old San Francisco Giants T-shirt, she mused that she wasn't Devin Isle, cocaptain of the cheerleading team anymore. She was just Devin. What a relief.

Devin picked up a squishy, sleepy Emerald from her bed and held her tight. The warm buzz of the cat was exactly what she needed. She closed her eyes and imagined that she was hugging Josh instead. It had been so long since they'd seen each other in person, she was starting to forget that he was three-dimensional.

Devin curled up tighter with Emerald and wondered what Josh was doing right now, on a Friday night. She realized that she had absolutely no idea. Cheerleading had been distracting her so much, she'd let things slip with him.

It was time to take action and get things between them back to normal. Starting now. Devin grabbed her cell, then found Josh's name. She hit Call. It rang three times and went straight to a familiar recording of him singing a song he called "No One Listens to Voice Mail Anymore." Devin didn't leave a message for obvious reasons. She brought up a text instead.

Where r u? Can we chat? I miss u & need u. <3 devver

She dropped her head back onto her pillow and waited patiently. A few moments later, her cell phone buzzed on the bed. She looked at the screen, hoping that it was from Josh. But it was only from Kate:

> You seemed stressed tonight @ the game and I wanted to tell you that I'm glad you're on the team! Xx Kate

She groaned. She had forgotten that she still had to break the news about her departure to the other girls on the team. Hopefully, Chloe would just do it for her at practice on Monday. But then Devin felt guilty.

Kate deserved to know now, since she had always been the nicest and most welcoming. They'd confided in each other about boys, and Kate was the one who'd invited her out with the other girls. Devin tapped away at the screen, doing her best to keep her response short.

> Thx k8—it's been fun...But I just quit.
> Thx for helping me out this year & good luck @ Regionals.
> U deserve to win.—dev

Where was Josh? She tried to remember if he'd mentioned his plans during their last conversation, but could come up with nothing. All she remembered was whining to him about her troubles with Chloe and the routine challenge. Why hadn't she let him talk? Suddenly her mind was racing with elaborate scenarios of what he could be doing right this minute.

Devin imagined Josh at the movies holding hands with that girl from his English class, Caroline Brett, or out at the bowling alley with Brittany Weaver. She pictured him in the back room of a party, kissing Wendy Easton, the most gorgeous girl at Spring Park High School. But Devin knew that her mind was just playing tricks on her. She logged on to her laptop and attempted to push the thoughts of everything away by watching an old rerun of *Modern Family*.

But after twenty minutes had passed with no response from her boyfriend, Devin suddenly felt very far away and helpless. All she wanted was to be back at her old home, away from Northside High, and near the one person who could make her feel better. If he would still have her, that was.

The emergency credit card called to Devin from the little purple box on her desk. She knew that when her dad had given it to her, he'd meant it was only for actual emergencies, but this really felt like one. Devin pulled up the Greyhound bus website on her computer and quickly selected a round-trip ticket from Sunny Valley to Spring Park. She entered all the card information and clicked Purchase before she had a chance to doubt herself.

Her mom was just settling down in front of a movie in

the living room when Devin walked out with her cheer duffel bag packed up. "And where do you think you're going, missy?" Linda asked with a smile. "Don't you want to watch *Under the Tuscan Sun* with me?"

"Last-minute cheer slumber party at Chloe's house!" Devin lied. "We're going to watch old Northside competition videos of her siblings to get ready for Regionals."

"How fun!" Linda said. "Do you want to take some of Sage's, too? Do you need a ride? Are you supposed to bring a snack to share?"

Devin held up her hands in protest. "No, thank you!" She headed to the door, eager to make her escape before her mom could ask any more questions. "Oh, and Mom?"

"Yes, honey?" Linda looked up again.

"I may stay at Chloe's tomorrow night, too. Major cocaptain planning session." She nodded as if that would prove she was telling the truth.

"Okay! I'll be at the hospital tomorrow anyway. Text me to check in so I know you're alive!" Linda chirped as Devin skipped out into the night. That had been pretty easy. Now if all went according to plan, she'd be at Josh's house by morning and her mom would never know the difference. Devin Isle was back to her old ways, pulling stunts completely by herself.

CHAPTER 26

The familiar sights of Spring Park came into view as the bus pulled over a hill. The first thing Devin saw was the old gas station that, improbably, made the best deli sandwiches in town. It was simply called Mart. When she was younger, Devin and her dad would grab lunch there before going to the park or taking a hike on the nearby trails. She could practically taste the turkey and mustard and was instantly nostalgic for this town and everything in it. It was filled with happy memories. It was her real home. She was glad to be there, even if it was going to cost her big-time when she got back to Sunny Valley.

By the time she arrived at the Spring Park bus station, it

was almost five in the morning. Her dad would be really excited to see her, but she doubted the reunion would be as sweet if she woke him up to come get her at this hour. A few taxis were parked in the lot, waiting for passengers. She climbed inside a neon-green one that said SPRING PARK AND RIDE and gave the driver directions.

Fifteen minutes later, after handing the driver a crumpled ten-dollar bill, Devin was finally home. A flood of feelings rushed back and she fought the urge to cry. It would be dumb to wake Alex Isle with sobs after all the trouble she had taken to get here on her own.

Devin felt around the bushes for the little blue Tupperware in which they used to hide the key. Thankfully, it was still there. She crept inside. The house was quiet and still, and the sky outside was about to begin its slow transition to light. It was so calm.

❋

"Devin, wake up.... Your mother nearly had a heart attack when she found out you were missing." Devin's dad spoke softly as he nudged his daughter awake. Devin rubbed her eyes sleepily and positioned herself upright. "Dad?" It felt like she'd just sat down on her favorite cushy tan sofa a few minutes ago, but it was clear by the bright daylight that she'd been knocked out for at least a few hours.

Devin blinked and glanced around the house. Everything looked the same except for the lack of a few choice decorative items that Linda had snagged before she moved out. Her dad, however, looked a little older than the last time she'd seen him. Stressed. His salt-and-pepper hair was more on the salt side of the spectrum. But his handsome face remained the same.

"Well, I can't say I'm not happy to see you, but you'd better explain yourself, kiddo." Alex Isle collapsed onto the sofa next to his younger daughter.

"Dad, I'm sorry for showing up like this. I just missed you so much!" Devin reached around and pulled him into a tight hug. "I had to come up here."

"I've missed you, too, but you can't run off like that by yourself. You're only fourteen! That was very dangerous." He gave her his best stern-father look. But she knew he wasn't really mad at her.

"I know...." Devin pulled her knees up to her chin. Being in this house again made her feel five years old. "So Mom knows?"

"Well, she called me in a panic! I guess she went over to your friend Chloe's house to bring some of Sage's cheerleading videos and snacks for you, but no one knew what she was talking about."

"Whoops," Devin said. The plan had seemed smarter and more well thought out last night. In all the excitement, Devin had completely forgotten to line up an alibi.

"Whoops is right." Alex stood up from the sofa and reached his hand out to help her up. "I've booked you a spot on a Monday morning bus back to Sunny Valley. Since you're already here, you might as well enjoy the weekend, before you are grounded for the rest of your life. What do you want to do first? You name it."

Devin looked up with the childlike expression she employed only with her dad, specifically when she wanted something. "Anything I want, really?"

❋

"So you're a big-time cheerleader now, just like your sister," Alex Isle observed, sipping his chocolate milk shake as he drove his black Subaru down a shady, oak-lined suburban street.

"Was," Devin said, drinking her strawberry milk shake. "I just quit on Friday."

"Is that so? Your mom didn't mention that part," Alex replied. "I don't know whether to comfort or congratulate you."

"She doesn't know yet," Devin replied matter-of-factly. "There it is!"

They parked across from a little brown cottage at the end of the block. The Griffith residence. It had been four months since the last time Devin had seen Josh. A little part of her was worried that when he saw her again he'd somehow change his mind about how he felt. She sat there for a few minutes, immobilized.

"Are you sure you don't want to just go knock on the door, sweetie?" Alex Isle prompted. He was one of those dads who tried his best, but he was clearly mystified by his teenage daughter.

"No, no." Devin shook her head. "I have a better idea!" She flipped her bag over her shoulder and pulled out her cell phone, typing up a quick, cryptic text.

josh, go outside!—devver

Thirty seconds later, Devin caught her breath as she saw her supercute boyfriend walk out onto the porch. He was wearing a sky-blue shirt and jeans, and hadn't even bothered to unstrap his guitar off his back. He looked at his phone in confusion, and then around the front yard. Finally, his eyes landed on Mr. Isle's car and who was inside.

Josh's eyes grew wide and his jaw dropped. "No way!" He started toward the car. Devin opened the door and ran outside, unable to contain her excitement any longer. She jogged over to meet him halfway and jumped straight into his arms with a shriek.

Josh caught her and swung her around the front-yard path, laughing. "Devver! What are you doing here?" Josh shouted. "Man, I can't believe this!"

"I ran away!" Devin jumped up and down, smiling.

"Seriously? But what about—?" Josh said, pointing to Devin's dad sitting in the car. Alex Isle waved at Josh and gave a friendly smile.

"Well, not really... I just kind of escaped! From Sunny Valley. For a few days." Devin squealed and gave him another quick hug. "Anyway, I had to see you. I had to tell you something in person. Not on a video screen."

Josh grabbed her hand and sat down on the porch step. "And what's that?" He grinned. Devin took a deep breath and looked at him. It was such a relief to see him in real life.

Devin squeezed his hand and took a moment to find the words. "I just wanted to say that... I'm sorry. For lying to you. For getting so caught up in my new life and friends. About everything, really." She looked down at her hands and fidgeted with the hem of her shirt.

"I'm sorry, too, Devin," Josh confessed, his voice serious. "But I can't forgive you... and I think that we should break up."

Devin looked up at him, tears forming in her eyes. "Really?"

Josh hesitated a moment before grabbing her and squeezing her tight. "Of course not, you crazy girl! I'm only kidding! I could never just ditch a catch like you!"

"You jerk!" Devin laughed, a wayward tear running down her cheek.

"Call it even?" Josh joked, standing up from the stone step and reaching out for her.

"Deal," Devin agreed, and took his hand.

Josh put his arm around her and walked her slowly back to her dad's car. "So now that that's all out of the way...is your dad taking us for pizza, or what?"

"Only if we can get a root beer with it."

CHAPTER 27

By the time Monday afternoon had rolled around, the news of Devin's departure had still somehow managed to remain a secret from most of the team, including Coach Steele. That much was obvious from the way she glanced down at her watch again and looked over to the gym door.

"Ooooooh, Devin's gonna get a demerit—she's more than half an hour late!" Marcy said, looking up at the big clock on the gym wall.

"Coach Steele is pissed." Leila smiled. "Look at her." The coach was clenching her jaw.

"It's only her first offense," said Emily, shutting Marcy

and Leila up. She was getting tired of Leila, her lackeys, and their constant negativity. It was as if they were only having fun when some sort of drama was going down.

"I'm sure she has a good reason for not being here," Kate said. All weekend, she'd made attempts to call Devin, who wasn't picking up her cell. Kate had hoped to convince Devin to stay, but she never got to talk to her. And Chloe claimed to know nothing about it, although Kate suspected otherwise, due to Chloe's lack of surprise at Devin's absence.

"Besides, missing one practice is not *that* big a deal," Emily said, crossing her arms over her chest. At least she hoped it wasn't. Just last night, Travis had let Emily know that Hashtag was going to record some of their original songs one day after school next week. They wanted Emily to sing on some of the tracks, and she couldn't say no to the opportunity, even if it meant missing a cheer practice.

"It is when you're the captain and there are only three practices left before Regionals," said Lexi. "The most important competition of the fall."

Chloe paced back and forth, her legs looking tanned and stronger than ever in her blue camp shorts. The squad had just done an intense round of conditioning, ending with ten laps around the gym. "I think we should all just focus on what we can do without Devin here. Maybe we should re-arrange some formations in case she doesn't show again?"

"You actually think she's not gonna show?" asked Emily. "Seems kind of unlike her. Normally she's all like, 'Try this stunt' and 'Do this incredibly hard tumbling pass.'" Emily attempted a Devin impression as she said it.

"I don't think she's coming, you guys," Chloe said. Maybe she should just tell everyone what she knew: that Devin was never coming back. Deep down, Chloe felt a little guilty. She'd been acting hot and cold to Devin all season, but it was too late for regrets now. They would just have to rechoreograph some of the routine and tumbling passes.

"That's enough conditioning, girls! Let's get started without Devin," Coach shouted to the team.

"But the routine will be entirely messed up without her!" Jenn yelled back. "How are we supposed to get the choreography timing right during the line formation if she's missing?"

"Count it out, Jenn. Do your best. We don't have time to wait anymore. But if she's not here in fifteen, I'm calling her mother."

Everyone ran to the center of the mat and took their opening positions. Coach Steele plugged in her iPod to the sound system and cued up Chloe's music, a superfast pop remix featuring Carly Rae Jepsen songs and a few current club hits. There were special sound effects edited into the song, strategically placed during each major stunt. The noises helped to amplify the visuals and keep the girls on track with their timing throughout the routine.

"Make this one count, girls!" There was an edge to her voice that made everyone very nervous. When Coach's voice sounded like that, they knew it was going to be a tough practice. She was definitely taking out her concern about Devin on the rest of the team.

As soon as the song began, half of the girls started doing the dance choreography in the center. They lifted their arms and swayed to the beat, spinning around to the back and then looking over their right shoulders in unison. The remaining girls launched themselves across the front of the mat from both sides into a round-off back handspring tumbling pass. The formation already looked lopsided, as Devin was supposed to be on the right side. They had only got through five more eight-counts of the music when Coach turned it off. She made a "cut" motion with her right hand and shook her head in defeat.

"Stop, stop! This isn't working. We should practice the stunt sequences before we run it with music. At least we can do those without her." Devin usually stayed up front doing back tucks and holding up the signs or megaphones during the stunts, anyway.

Chloe nodded in agreement. "From the top of the cheer, everyone!" She could totally handle this on her own. She clapped her hands a few times as encouragement. But no one was listening. Several girls ran to their bags to get drinks of water and others just started chatting.

"Chloe, I have to step out," Coach Steele shouted to the captain, a phone to her ear. She was probably calling Linda Isle to grill her about Devin. "Don't start till I get back," she warned, pointing her finger at the girls.

Across the mat, Jenn and Lexi sat facing each other in a straddle position, stretching and whispering. Carley and Kalyn leaned against the wall, talking in hushed tones. Everyone seemed to be trying to put together what had happened to Devin. Or they were just using it as an excuse to take a break.

"HEY!" Chloe shouted again, and everyone looked up from their little conversations. "Didn't you guys hear me? I said—*from the top of the cheer*!" Chloe threw her arms up in exasperation. "I want to go over the stunt sequences and make some changes. Now." She raised her eyebrows expectantly.

Kate frowned at her. "But Coach isn't even in the gym, Chlo. She said to wait."

"It'll be fine. We have to use every minute of practice we're given," she replied, beginning to get annoyed at the apathetic attitudes of her team.

"Chloe, you of all people know that we could get in major trouble," Kate said, searching her friend's face in confusion. It was unlike Chloe to go against the AACCA guidelines. Her whole identity was tied up in being the perfect cheerleader who knew all the rules and abided by them.

But Chloe didn't care about the rule book at this moment. She was getting frustrated with the lack of energy in the gym. Did this team want to win or not? From the way they were all lazing around on their butts, joking with one another and gossiping about stupid things, it certainly seemed like the latter. Even her best friend, Emily, who was supposed to support her, was standing in the corner texting. Chloe bet that the girls at Breckenridge High were in the middle of completing multiple toe touch basket tosses at this very moment.

Something drastic needed to be done.

Chloe ran over to the bleachers and found the silver whistle sitting on top of Coach Steele's action plan binder, under a stack of signed medical release forms for Regionals. She brought the cold metal to her lips and blew as hard as she could.

Fweeeeeeeeeeet!

The high-pitched noise rang throughout the gym and everyone snapped to attention, thinking it was Coach Steele. Chloe smiled, satisfied. "Good. Now that I have your attention, I just want to remind you all why you're here."

Chloe held up the action plan binder like it was the Ten Commandments. It was covered in snapshots of their team at the football games throughout the season, smiling and stunting on the sidelines. "Let's turn to today's schedule, shall we?" She flipped through the pages and landed on the current date. She cleared her throat and read aloud, "Ah, Monday, November tenth—POLISH ROUTINE FOR REGIONALS!" She slammed the binder shut like she'd made her point and put it back on the bench.

Chloe climbed up onto the bleachers so that she stood high above everyone else.

"Come on, Wolves! We can't choke now!" Chloe pleaded. "This is our time to shine—competition is entirely about *our* skills. *Our* hard work! *Our* amazing sport!" She stopped and pointed at them. "And it *is* a sport. Don't you want to prove yourselves among your peers?"

Slowly, the girls started to stand up from the mat, their muscles already stiff from the short break. They knew she was right.

"But we're never going to beat the Bulldogs," Kalyn said, motioning to her fellow teammates. A few of them nodded. "They're way too good, Chloe. We know that."

"And we're okay with it," Arianna said, still sitting cross-legged on the mat.

"Well, I'm not!" Chloe proclaimed defiantly. She hopped down from the bleachers in one graceful motion. Her cheer shoes squeaked on the basketball court floor. "I have been waiting since I was twelve years old to wear a Northside Timberwolves uniform and compete at Nationals. Regionals is our only shot to get a bid to go there. So let's not waste it!" Chloe looked to her teammates to back her up. "And don't forget what Coach said about the program getting cut. She was serious."

"I thought that was just a thing she said to motivate us," Carley said. "They are really cutting half of the team next year?"

Chloe nodded. "It's true." She wasn't really sure if it was, but if Coach had used it to inspire everyone, then so could she.

"You know what I say to that?" Chloe shouted. "TIMBER, TIMBER, TIMBER!" She clapped her hands together.

"WOLVES!" they all shouted together, getting pumped up.

Coach still wasn't back, but soon they were focused on the stunt from the cheer section of their routine.

"And five. Six. Seven. Eight," Chloe counted off as the girls began to go through the motions again. Chloe's version of the sequence, which they were now practicing, was a very watered-down version of Devin's—meaning it was much easier. Basically, it didn't include the twisting full up, and instead of featuring a heel stretch pyramid, there was a regular pyramid. Chloe's sequence also included a few of her favorite shoulder sits—a simple stunt where one girl sits atop another's shoulders. The whole thing was designed to hit every time. And it did.

There was only one problem: it was really boring. As she and her teammates ran through the moves, it even felt boring. They knew it didn't look nearly impressive enough to wow the judges. They needed to do something amazing. They needed to do Devin's sequence. With the heel stretch pyramid.

Just as Chloe was about to suggest this to the group, a cell phone ring echoed throughout the gym. "Can someone take care of that?" Chloe groaned. Everyone knew cell phones weren't allowed during practice, but Coach wasn't in the room.

"Whoops, sorry!" Emily said, jogging over to her bag to turn it off. But when she looked down at the caller ID, it said TRAVIS HOLLISTER. He never called her, saying he was a strictly text-only guy. It must have been something really important. "I really have to take this! BRB!" she shouted as she ran toward the exit and through the door.

Great, Chloe thought. *Now we've lost our main top girl, too.*

❋

Once outside, Emily hit Accept Call and answered eagerly. "What's up, dude? Something wrong?" She began to pace around, shielding her eyes from the late fall sunshine.

"No, not at all!" Travis said, his voice cheerful. "Totally the opposite, actually!"

"Really?" Emily responded. "What is it, then?"

"Nic Aragon is interested in Hashtag! He wants us to record on Saturday at SV Studios in LA!" Travis practically yelled. "And he demanded that you be there to sing with us, too."

"Are you serious?" Emily screamed into the receiver. "Wow! Omigod, yes! I'll be there!" She sprang up and down as if she were on a trampoline instead of concrete.

"Heck, yes!" Travis replied. "So I'll send you the info and I'll see you then. Make sure your voice gets some rest!"

"Of course!" said Emily, feeling herself bubble over with excitement at the prospect of recording for a real record label. An important one. "Talk to you later!"

She clicked off her phone and was about to let out a squeal of excitement when she suddenly realized that she already had plans on Saturday—*unchangeable* plans. Regionals. What was she going to tell Travis? Or what would she tell the squad? Either way, she'd be letting a group of people down and sacrificing their dreams—not to mention her own.

Emily had hardly begun to process the unfortunate coincidence of having the two most important events of her life clash, when she heard a scream come from inside the gym.

Emily ran back inside to see the entire team huddled around someone lying on the mat. She couldn't make out who it was, but Coach Steele was also rushing toward the group, concern spread across her face.

When Emily reached them, she almost couldn't believe her eyes. Chloe was horizontal on the mat, wincing in pain and holding her ankle.

"What happened?" Coach Steele barked at the squad, kneeling down to inspect Chloe's injury. It looked like a pretty bad sprain, maybe even a fracture. It was already swelling up and beginning to turn purple.

"She made us try a new stunt with her," Gemma explained, her voice shaky. "She insisted on being top girl to demonstrate, but we couldn't hold her and..."

"We tried to tell her!" Leila said, jutting her hip out and looking annoyed. "Chloe hasn't practiced being a top girl since we were kids."

"Oh, Chloe..." Coach said, full of disappointment. "Stunting without a spotter? In a different position than you're used to? What were you thinking?"

"I was thinking..." Chloe whimpered. Big, watery tears began to fall down her cheeks as the realization of what had just happened set in. "I was thinking...I just thought I could do it myself."

❋

Though her mom tried to comfort her, Chloe wouldn't say a single word on the way home from the doctor's office. All she could do was stare out the window and try to wish away the events of the past few hours. She had been so foolish. If she could take everything back, she would. Starting with the attempt to do the stunt in the first place, followed by her brilliant idea to try it as the top girl, since Emily was outside on the phone—and finally the part where she'd sat and listened to Dr. Stephenson explain that under *no* circumstances was she to compete at Regionals. Chloe was supposed to stay off her badly sprained ankle for two full weeks. If she wanted it to heal correctly, that was.

"Well, at least it didn't happen before Nationals," Joanie Davis said, turning onto their street. "You can still compete in the spring if the team places this weekend."

It was hard not to hate herself a little. Chloe's ego had been getting in her way all season with Devin and it had taken over today at practice. She had no one to blame but herself. But her mom's last comment had given her an idea. If she couldn't lead the squad as captain at Regionals, she was going to find them someone who could. Her team deserved that much. And if they succeeded, Chloe might even get a chance at competition with the team at Nationals.

Chloe pulled out her cell phone and brought up Devin Isle in her contacts list. She made the message short enough to pique Devin's curiosity. She hoped it would be enough to garner a response.

Devin—I'm sorry 4 evrything. Call me tonite. It's an emergency.—Chloe

CHAPTER 28

When Devin received the cryptic text message from Chloe on Monday night, she had been hiding in her room back in Sunny Valley, like Anne Boleyn awaiting her sentence in the Tower of London. She'd just gotten home from the bus station and followed her mother's directions to go straight home and to her room. Even though Devin had enjoyed her two days of relaxation up north, she felt a deep sense of dread at the lecture she was about to get. Linda was angry. Now Devin was desperately trying to think of ways to explain exactly what had compelled her to forfeit the cocaptainship, quit the cheerleading team, and run away on a Greyhound bus to see her boyfriend, who lived seven hours away. Even she could acknowledge that it all was really irresponsible.

Devin stared at the text message for a good five minutes before deciding that she wanted to hear what Chloe Davis had to say. She had said it was an emergency, after all.

After a brief conversation in which Chloe broke the news of her injury and asked Devin to come back to the team, Devin didn't give her an answer. She hung up, sat back, and thought about her options.

At least the long bus ride to Spring Park and back had already given Devin a lot of time to think about the team. As she watched the California landscape fly by, she'd thought about everything that had gone down during this crazy season. Sure, it had been filled with team drama and long hours of practice, but it was all sort of exciting when she really considered it. Cheerleading had helped her to adjust to life at Northside High. It was kind of hard to be down on a place that you spent hours yelling great things about. Plus, Devin had even made a few friends, like Kate and Emily. The positives outweighed the negatives.

And when Devin opened up about everything to Josh over lunch on Saturday, his response had really surprised her. "So why did you quit again?" he'd asked her, scarfing a piece of pepperoni pizza at her favorite Italian place, Giovanni's. "Because some other girl thought she was better than you and tried to get you kicked off the team?"

"Exactly," replied Devin. "No one wants me there."

"That's the silliest thing I ever heard you say, Devver," Josh had said. "Of course they do—the team elected you as their captain after only knowing you for a week! That's got to count for something."

Somehow, even though Coach Steele had told her the same exact thing, Devin hadn't really believed it until now. Josh's words had reminded her that she'd completely abandoned the team, too—it wasn't just Chloe who was affected by this. That changed things a bit.

Before she'd kissed him good-bye at the bus station, Josh had reassured her that he didn't really care about the fact that she was a cheerleader now. In fact, he thought it was sorta cool that she'd put herself out there like that.

Devin made Chloe wait an hour before calling her back, even though she knew her answer right away. "Okay, I'll do it—I'll come back to the team. I mean, as long as my mom lets me."

"You will?" Chloe sounded extremely relieved. "Omigod, thank you. The team is a mess and—"

"Under one condition..." Devin said.

"Anything!" Chloe replied, not wasting a second.

"You have to answer a question." Devin hesitated. It was time to clear the air once and for all. "Someone on the team showed me an e-mail you sent where you were trying to get me kicked off the squad. I just have to know, why did you do that? Did you really hate me that much?"

"What are talking about? What e-mail? Who?" Chloe asked, rapid-fire. "And, no, of course I don't hate you."

Devin considered not giving up her source, but decided that if Leila had lied to her, she didn't really owe her anything. "Leila Savett showed me the e-mail," Devin said.

Chloe scoffed, "Well, I never wrote anything like that."

"You didn't?" Devin had been holding on to the notion for so long, using it as fuel against Chloe. It was odd to think it might have just been a doctored letter that Leila had written purely for Devin's benefit. Devin realized it had probably never even been sent to anyone. "Now that I think of it, it didn't really sound like you wrote it. You're much smarter than that."

"Well, Leila told *me* that *you* were walking around saying awful things about me to the other squad members, hoping to undermine me and get them to hate me," Chloe said. "I don't suppose that's true, either?"

"Are you kidding me?" Devin suddenly broke into laughter and Chloe joined in. It all seemed really silly now.

Chloe was in awe of Leila's entire thinly veiled plot and her own inability to see it. "Man, how did we fall for her lies?"

"We weren't exactly trying to get along this entire

season," Devin said. "I think we were looking for reasons to fight. I guess people really do only hear what they want to hear."

"You know what I want to hear now?" Chloe asked. "'First place goes to the Northside High School JV Timberwolves.'"

"You know what? Me too," agreed Devin.

CHAPTER 29

The air was crisp and bright on a beautiful Southern California fall day. Two yellow school buses waited out by the Northside High School front entrance even though it was early on a Saturday morning. The long windows of each bus were decorated in royal-blue paint and bubble letters of encouragement. They said GO, NORTHSIDE CHEER! on one side and REGIONALS, HERE WE COME! on the other. Big blue-and-gold construction-paper stars, one with each cheerleader's name and graduation year on it, were taped to the insides of the windows. It was lucky that the bus was yellow—it really made the Northside colors pop!

It was a tradition for all of the girls to meet at school

and ride to the competition together on the bus. Their families would follow shortly after to settle into the audience bleachers at the competition venue. The bus ride was the perfect way for the girls to bond as a team and get pumped up right before their performance that afternoon.

The parking lot was filling up fast with parents' cars, there to drop off their daughters for the big day. Many of the windows of the vehicles also showed support for the NHS cheerleaders. There were homemade signs, pennants, and bumper stickers everywhere. Kate's mom had even allowed her to decorate their minivan with some glittery NHS decals and a Timberwolf antenna ball. The MacDonald family pulled into the lot and Kate climbed out from the far backseat, squeezing past her little siblings' car seats. She smoothed down her uniform and stretched her body out. Her long legs really weren't designed to fit back there comfortably.

"Good morning, MacDonalds!" Coach Steele shouted with a smile. "Kate, you're on Bus A with the other JV girls. Hurry it up!"

"Bye, Mom! Bye, Dad! See you guys after!" Kate slung her duffel bag over her shoulder and skipped toward her coach, beginning to feel giddy with nervous excitement. The moment she stepped onto the bus, she was filled with pride in her school and pride in being one of its cheerleaders.

It was inspiring to see her teammates all decked out in

their uniforms. The girls looked polished with their hair braided perfectly into their ponytails and their competition makeup on. They looked like champions. Down the row, each girl was chatting with her seatmate and laughing. Even though they'd had a rocky season, Kate could tell that everyone was feeling really hopeful. It was contagious.

"Kate! Over here!" Devin waved. Her curls had been smoothed and tamed into the sleek diagonal braid. "I saved you a seat next to me."

"Thanks!" Kate replied, sliding in beside her. "So did you get in a lot of trouble for going up to the Bay?"

"Actually, yeah," Devin admitted, taking in the scene. "It sucks, but it was worth it. At least my mom is letting me perform today after everything I did."

Kate put her hand on Devin's shoulder. "You've done a lot of good stuff this year, too. I'm sure she can see that," Kate said sincerely. "All of us can."

"Thanks, Kate," Devin replied, feeling really lucky. "Can you believe Regionals are finally here? I just hope we're ready."

"Don't worry, Dev. We are," Kate chirped. "Anyway, we have to be."

Devin took a deep breath. She hoped Kate was right.

The bus began to pull out of the parking lot, and all the girls leaned toward the windows to wave good-bye to their parents. Once they turned onto the road, Jenn stood up in her seat and led everyone in a round of "Timber-, Timber-, Timber-wolves!"

✺

"Welcome, girls! How can I help?" A smiling brunette in a light blue UCA polo shirt sat at a folding table near the doors of the practice room. The table was littered with stacks of paperwork and Regional Championships programs. It bore a large banner that said WELCOME TO UCA REGIONALS!

"We're just checking in," Devin replied, taking in the sight of the masses of uniformed girls flitting about the giant room in color-coded groups like schools of tropical fish in a reef. The sounds of battling cheers attacked her ears from all directions. Everywhere she looked, there were bows, short skirts, and white cheer shoes. The ponytails seemed even higher and fancier than usual and the makeup was even more extreme.

Devin couldn't believe she was at the UCA Regional High School Cheerleading Championships despite the events of the past week. Heck, the events of the past year! So much had changed. The old Devin would have whined and complained if she had had to *watch* Sage perform at one of these things. And now here she stood, wearing her own newly washed NHS uniform, sparkly gold makeup, and a poufy white bow in her fiery-red braided ponytail.

"Northside High School. Junior Varsity division." Devin motioned to the team behind her, decked out in their crisp blue-and-gold uniforms. They were busy sizing up the competition. It was easy to psych yourself out if you studied the other teams too much, so she hoped to keep the girls close and focused until they went on.

"Welcome! Are you the captain?" the woman chirped.

It took Devin a moment to respond because she was really distracted by a huge swarm of girls wearing yellow uniforms and shouting, "GO, HORNETS! Bzzzz! GO, HORNETS! Bzzzz!" repeatedly as they passed by.

"Yes—Devin Isle?" Devin scanned the roster on the table for her name.

The woman perked up immediately. "You wouldn't happen to be the baby sister of Sage Isle, would you?"

Devin flushed red. "Yep, that's me . . . Sage's little sister." She could never escape it, especially in a setting like this. But maybe it would actually work to her advantage this time.

"What a treat to have you here!" the woman replied warmly. "Sage was one of our favorite All-American team members when she was a senior! That girl could really light up a room with her energy. Such a great cheerleader. You'll tell her hi from Sandy for me?" The woman handed over a stack of paperwork and programs and had Devin sign her name.

"Of course!" Devin smiled back, but she knew she was going to forget the woman's name in an hour. She had so much going through her head at the moment.

Sandy spoke up again. "All members of your team are present, right? Because you're not supposed to sign this one until they are." She tapped the paper in front of her.

"Definitely," Devin lied. They were all there except for Emily, who'd insisted that she wanted to be driven to the convention center by her brother instead of taking the bus with everyone else. Devin was sure that she would be there soon.

"And your coach?" Sandy asked, raising her eyebrows.

"She's on the other bus with the Varsity girls. Should be here any minute," Devin answered, itching to go join the rest of her team and start warming up.

The woman smiled. "Great! You guys go on at two forty-five, right after Ricker High School." She pointed to a small squad in the corner wearing green-and-white uniforms. "That's them right there. Make sure you're all ready backstage. If we call your team more than twice, you can't go on." Her face got very serious. "I mean it—you can't go on."

"Okay, got it! Well, I think we're set!" Devin replied, and then she scurried over to join her teammates. She expected them to be chatting and laughing like usual, but everyone was stretching and warming up in dead silence.

Just as she'd been worried about—seeing the competition was psyching them out. Devin looked around, and instantly spotted Breckenridge High across the room. Their teal-and-white-and-orange uniforms were unmistakable. They looked as polished as ever, but this time their team makeup even included little teal rhinestone paw-print tattoos on their cheeks.

A couple of the girls stood with their legs stretched completely flat against the wall in a standing split. A few others were practicing their scorpions by stretching their legs high behind them and grabbing their feet. Their captain, the tall and pretty Karen Gelb, who was currently running through a high-level jump combination with ease, mesmerized Devin. Her black ponytail swung in the air with each toe touch and side hurdler. When she was finished, she looked up directly at Devin and waved. Devin looked away sharply. She'd had no idea Karen had spotted her.

Maybe this was why Sage had told her not to watch any of the other teams. She turned her focus back to her own. "Okay, team. Let's just, um, keep stretching until Coach Steele gets here. Good work."

Devin ditched her bag and found a spot on the ground next to Kate. She sat down and stretched into a wide straddle position, leaning forward. "So what's up with you and Adam, then?" Devin asked, grasping for any topic except the present situation. "Is he coming to watch you kick butt today?"

Kate looked embarrassed. She always forgot that out of everyone, Devin probably knew the most about her and Adam's little...whatever it was. "He wanted to, but I don't think we're quite there yet," she admitted shyly. "Besides, I'm still figuring out whether or not I even want a boyfriend right now. We all just started high school, you know?" Her long brown hair and thick, dark eyelashes and big eyes made her look so innocent. Especially when she made statements like that.

Kate took some Vaseline out of her bag and started to apply a little bit to her teeth. It was an old beauty-pageant trick that reminded you to smile. She handed the tub over to Devin and continued. "I guess I just want to enjoy it without obsessing over anything too much. I have a tendency to worry."

"I hadn't noticed at all," Devin teased. Kate poked her bottom lip out a little. "Only kidding." She wiped some Vaseline onto her teeth and winced in disgust. "I actually think that's really smart. Trust me—having a boyfriend is a lot of work," Devin admitted. "Especially when it's long-distance."

"Are you guys going to try to stay together?" Kate asked.

"Who knows what the future holds?" Devin said, smiling. It was the truth. She and Josh were still trying to figure out whether or not to hold on to the special thing they had between them, despite the distance. It wasn't going to be an overnight decision.

"Hey!" Chloe said, hobbling up on a pair of crutches. "Coach Steele wanted me to come back here and wish you guys luck." She was wearing her uniform, her strawberry-blond locks tied up and everything, like a true-blue member of the squad. She looked pretty bummed, but was doing her best to put on a brave face.

"Chloe!" Kalyn exclaimed, and the girls began to crowd around her, offering their sympathies for her hurt ankle. They all knew how much she cared about the team and how bad she must be feeling right now.

After delivering a few choice words of encouragement, Chloe realized something was off. "Hey, does anyone know where Emily is?"

Kalyn raised her hand cautiously. "I may have an idea...."

"All right...where is she, Kay?"

"I overheard her saying something to that Travis Hollister guy about a recording session in LA with Hashtag this morning," Kalyn said. "I think she was planning to come here straight after?"

"What?" Devin said, picturing Emily sitting on a gridlocked freeway somewhere. "This is a disaster. How could she do this to us?"

"Well, I hate to stick up for Emily and point this out— but you did the same thing with your little dramatic exit and jaunt up to the Bay, right?" Leila said. Her face was overly made up, and her smoky eyeliner looked a little rac- coonish. "You're hardly the picture-perfect team member yourself."

"And you are?" Chloe scoffed, hobbling over to Leila on her crutches and proceeding to stare her down as she spoke. "You want to tell the rest of the team how you've been messing with me and Devin all season, trying to make us hate each other so you could swoop right in?"

Leila narrowed her eyes and smiled. "I didn't even have to try to make you argue. You two did that entirely on your own. All I did was give you a little encouragement. I see no crime in that."

"Leila, get hold of yourself," Devin interjected. "As annoyed as I am with you right now, we have to be united as a team. Remember? Northside is counting on us to win this year."

"You're right," said Chloe. "Sorry, Devin."

"No worries. Now let's text-blast Emily and find her ASAP!"

✹

Thirty minutes later, a tall woman holding a clipboard tapped Devin on the shoulder. "Northside High School?

Get ready, you're up next." Devin turned to Kate and Chloe with a look of sheer panic on her face. Emily was still missing and she wasn't answering anyone's texts or calls.

Devin wasn't really sure what to do. They couldn't go on without her—yet they had to go on right now or risk being disqualified altogether. They had approximately two minutes and thirty seconds to figure out what do while Ricker High School was onstage. Time wasn't exactly on their side. They trudged over to the wings, hoping for some sort of answer to reveal itself before time ran out.

Ricker's music seemed somehow shorter than any of the other squads' before them. In what felt like just a few moments, the green-and-white-clad girls bounced off the mat and back into the wings, hugging one another and shrieking with delight.

"Ladies and gentlemen!" the host bellowed to the crowd. "All the way from Sunny Valley...the Northside High School JV Timberwoooolves!"

CHAPTER 30

"The Northside High School JV Timberwolves!"
the host repeated into the microphone, less enthusiastically
this time. Devin bit her lip anxiously. Her feet were glued
to the floor. What were they going to do? Her heart was
beating out of her chest with nerves and she couldn't think
of anything.

Devin was just preparing to approach the clipboard
woman to try to explain the situation, when Emily suddenly shot past them like a rocket. "I'm here! I'm here!" she
yelled, running straight onto the mat. She did a back handspring and pumped her index finger in the air. "Yeah,
Northside's number one!" No one on the team had time to

register what was happening, so they just followed her, running out and yelling "N-H-S!" or "Go, Timberwolves!" to pump up the crowd for the performance. Devin threw in a couple of backflips.

Adrenaline surged through her veins as she took her place—front and center. She did her best not to think about how many people were watching. Hundreds of cheerleading supporters sat in the bleachers, clapping and yelling for Northside. The massive NHS section was obvious from the sea of blue-and-gold-clad fans. Not to mention their loud cheers when the girls had run out from backstage. It was a rush unlike anything Devin had ever experienced.

Devin held her head high and smiled at the crowd. Nothing bad could happen out here. She had sixteen other girls with her—they were all there to support one another and cheer together.

Then Devin lowered her head, stared down at her white cheer shoes against the bright blue mat, and focused on her breathing. It might have been only ten seconds or so, but Devin waited for the crowd to settle before giving Coach Steele the signal to start the music. It was finally showtime.

Breathe, Devin thought. *Hit it. Just like at practice.*

Devin looked up, nodded her head twice, and finally the opening notes of their music began. The team sprang instantly into action, moving their bodies to the fast beat. They raised their arms up high and back down to their hips, sliding back and forth. The girls stretched down, and half the team rolled to the mat, while the rest remained standing. The song changed, and a segment of ultraquick arm movements all done perfectly in unison drew extra cheers from the crowd.

As they danced, they directed their attention at the crowd instead of at the judges like a lot of other squads had, including Breckenridge. This was Coach Steele's tip. She maintained that cheerleading was, above all, about getting the crowd excited, even when you were competing.

Devin headed to the corner of the mat along with Arianna, Jenn, and Leila. As soon as the group of girls in the middle finished their dance sequence, Devin shot across the mat like a rocket—completing a round-off, back handspring, full. The Northside cheering section went wild! The other tumblers shot across the mat after her. So far, everything had gone perfectly. The moment of truth came next—the stunts.

The song switched yet again, signaling the team to jog to their first stunting positions. They held their arms tight against their sides and counted to the music through wide smiles.

Backstage, Chloe held her breath. Could her teammates pull it off? "Come on, Wolves! WOOOO!" she hollered, aching to be out there with them. The least she could do was lend her vocal cords to the team.

Back on the mat, the NHS girls hit the full-up extensions, no problem. In the middle, Emily shot up into a liberty, switching her feet on the next count into her tic-tock, before being caught in a cradle. The crowd cheered like crazy. On the next eight-count, the two side groups tossed their girls up into basket tosses, just like they had practiced a million times.

Coach Steele jumped up and down, smiling and clapping. "That's it, ladies!"

With only one more element in the sequence to go, the girls were now seriously feeding off the intense energy of the crowd. They said the eight-counts in their heads as they lifted the top girls up one last time...into a perfectly executed heel stretch pyramid. They held it, smiling, as the music came to a halt.

The stunt groups caught their top girls in cradle dismounts and walked to their formation for the cheer section.

"ALL RIGHT!" Devin projected her voice into the crowd to begin the cheer. It actually felt strange not to be saying it with Chloe. All sixteen of the other girls snapped to attention in formation behind Devin. They moved their arms in an intricate pattern, being careful to keep their lines clean and their voices loud.

"NORTHSIDE FANS...IN THE STANDS. YELL BLUE...AND GOLD!" the girls cheered, and clapped their hands twice.

"YELL BLUE AND GOLD!" *Clap. Clap.*

"Blue and gold!" the Northside parents cheered. Even Joanie and Paul Davis were yelling out. Chloe found them in the crowd and she cheered along from the wings.

"COME ON, FANS, GET ON YOUR FEET!"

"LISTEN TO...THE NORTHSIDE BEAT!"

They demonstrated the "Northside beat" by clapping all together as they walked into a new formation. This time, Kate was front and center. But she was in the zone now. Nerves didn't even register anymore.

"WE SAY BLUE, YOU SAY GOLD!" Carley and Lexi held up brand-new glittering signs that said BLUE on one side and GOLD on the other as the rest of the girls prepped to do a series of jumps.

"BLUE!" Carley and Lexi reached their signs up, projecting their voices out into the crowd. "BLUE!" They flipped the signs over. "GOLD!" everyone shouted. "GOLD!"

"WE SAY WOLF PACK, YOU SAY FIGHT!"

"WOLF PACK!" the team yelled in unison, reaching their arms up to prep. Everyone except Carley and Lexi launched into a double toe touch. Kate hit it better than she had all semester.

"Fight!"

"WOLF PACK! FIGHT!"

The girls arranged themselves into a perfect formation of lines to get ready for the big finish. "NORTHSIDE, FIGHT! WOLF PACK, GROWL!"

All seventeen girls launched into standing back hand-springs at the same time. Then they popped back up and shouted to the fans, "OUR MIGHTY WOLF PACK'S ON THE PROWL!"

All during their cheer and final musical-dance section, they rode the wave of adrenaline they'd gotten from doing the stunts perfectly in the hardest part of the routine. From then on, the smiles on their faces were anything but fake. The girls had finally achieved what they had set out to do, and it couldn't have come together at a better time. When the last note of their music hit, all seventeen girls held their body positions, grinning from ear to ear, just soaking up the applause.

At the awards ceremony later on, the Northside Timberwolves sat cross-legged on the mat along with all the other squads who had competed that day. All the teams listened patiently as the competition announcer called each of the top squads up in order of their final ranking. Devin's heart had finally stopped racing, but she was still in awe of the crowds. She took it all in, reveling in the postperformance glow with her teammates. It was a satisfying conclusion to their weeks of hard work and dedication to practicing. Chloe had even made her way onto the mat in her uniform and crutches and was sitting between Devin and Kate.

"No matter what happens, I want you to know you totally rocked it out there today. The squad looked awesome," Chloe said to Devin, beaming. Chloe may not have performed that day, but she was still a part of the team. She even wore a pawprint tattoo on her face and a side French braid, just like the rest of them. In fact, the crowd-pleasing routine had been her creation, after all. Well, both hers and Devin's.

"Thanks, Chloe," Devin replied. Then she reached over and gave Chloe a quick hug. She wasn't sure if it was just the mix of adrenaline and endorphins, but she couldn't help feeling a camaraderie with her former rival. Chloe was right—the squad had performed amazingly well, and Devin was proud of what they'd accomplished. *I guess I really am a cheerleader now*, she thought, smiling.

"In third place...Breckenridge High!" the announcer exclaimed. The cavernous room erupted in claps and shouts of excitement. Everyone's spirits were high, and even the Northside girls joined in, although Devin realized that announcement probably meant their squad hadn't placed at all. She caught Coach Steele's eye and shrugged her shoulders, still grinning.

The announcer continued. "And in second place, we have...Northside High School! Congratulations, Northside!"

Devin's mouth dropped open in shock. All of the girls jumped up from their seats on the mat and began cheering loudly, bouncing up and down and hugging one another.

"Hey, Cocaptain!" Chloe yelled to Devin over the roar of the crowd and the chants of "N-H-S!" coming from their teammates. "Looks like we have to get working on our technique for Nationals!"

Devin smiled. "When do we start?"